I'll Remember You

TM FLETCHER

ISBN 978-1-63814-778-7 (Paperback)
ISBN 978-1-63814-779-4 (Digital)

This novel is entirely a work of fiction. The names, characters, and incidents portrayed in it are the work of the author's imagination.

Any resemblance to actual persons, living or dead, events, or localities is entirely coincidental.

T. M. Fletcher asserts the moral right to be identified as the author of this work.

T. M. Fletcher has no responsibility for the persistence or accuracy of URLs for external or third-party Internet websites referred to in this publication and does not guarantee that any content on such websites is, or will remain, accurate or appropriate.

Covenant Books, Inc.
11661 Hwy 707
Murrells Inlet, SC 29576
www.covenantbooks.com

To all those who dare to dream, never stop dreaming.

Contents

Chapter 1

June 1942

Why am I here? What am I going to do with my life? Where will I be in five years? Those are weighty questions every graduating senior ponders before that final walk into adulthood.

"Katie! Katie girl! Hey, when you bring your head out of the clouds, can I buy a pound of cod? I'd like some of that mackerel too! Is it fresh? Nothing like fresh mackerel!"

"Yes, sorry, Mr. Thomas." I reached in the display case where all the fresh catch of the day lay neatly placed on mounds of ice hours earlier. My father and brother ventured out before daylight, as they did every day. I grabbed a bunch of yesterday's newspapers and wrapped the fish tightly, brushing my hair back from my face and wiping my hands on my apron, still stained with the morning fish cleaning. A gruesome and smelly job, but I worked in the store as far back as I could remember, mostly in the kitchen with my mom, serving the local folks old family recipes that had been handed down for years.

"Thank you, Mr. Thomas! Tell your wife and Rebecca I said Hello." Rebecca is my best friend. Our families knew each other for many years.

Mr. Thomas turned to leave and turned back quickly as he held the door. "Give your mother and father our best."

Business had been a little slow. People started to ration, in preparation for what had already begun and would become worse, the war.

O'Leary's Fishery and Pub was a staple of the town for decades. Nothing fancy, just a corner storefront was a line of connected clothing stores, pawnshops, a drugstore, and Demetre Grocery. It had a worn, military blue exterior, two bay windows, on each side of the old wood door, with a sizable pane of glass. On the door, the name of the pub worn with time. They experienced good years, and more recently, declining business. I worried about what I would do if we lost the pub. I received word about some factory work that may be available soon. I found myself accustomed to hard work, so the manual labor and hot conditions didn't scare me. Although, I had also heard about a possible job opening at the naval shipyard in Charleston. That was quite a distance from here, which would mean I would have to possibly leave home and live in a boarding house or find a roommate. There were a lot of decisions I was not sure I was prepared for. But ready or not, they are coming at some point in my future. Being an adult began to look quite different from the romantic notions I had before now. "I should sit down, and talk with Rebecca about this."

I walked through the old wooden door behind the counter. There, Momma stood, preparing for the diners that would come in later, her dark auburn hair up in her usual messy bun, white apron, flour on her hands and face. Everything seemed to suddenly be in slow motion. The sun streamed through the windows, like she was on a movie set. The air looked soft and filtered the light, with flour flying through the air, swirling all around her. She was blissfully unaware while feverishly preparing the battered fish fillets for the day. What can I tell you about my momma? She is a quiet soul, kind, and giving of her time and heart. She tends to our elderly neighbors and to me and my brother and father every day, as regular as the sun and moon. She had a few brothers and sisters of her own; she was the youngest. They grew up during hard times. Many of them are gone now. She still has one sister and a brother living out West. Momma also loves music. That is where I get it from, I'm sure. In the evenings, Momma always makes time for herself by sitting at the old upright piano that is not quite in tune and plays after dinner. Many of the songs she plays are from her childhood in Ireland. It is so comforting and peaceful. We all sit quietly and listen from the porch, enjoying the evening. When the song comes to an end, she always smiles, with a satisfied look, like she completed a race, then back to the tasks that never seem to end.

Now my pops, he is strong and steadfast. I don't know of another person that works as hard or is more dedicated to his profession. He has one sister that is seven years older. She lives just up the coast, above Charleston, in Isle of Palm. Aunt Mags runs a bed and breakfast and had no children, so her nieces and nephews were her surrogate children. We love her, and her home is a magical place to visit. Pops and Aunt Mags are close, but that was not always the case. They have lived on the coast here in South Carolina for generations. He loves the sea, and it is his second love, next to my mother. He awakens in the early hours as the sun, with its beautiful pink and orange hues, begins peaking over the horizon. He loads his truck and grabs a thermos of coffee and heads to the docks for a long day on the water. Sometimes, I watch him standing, with his nets and thermos, gazing out over the dunes, taking a moment to soak in the beauty and peace of that early light before his busy and demanding day begins. I am thankful for the parents I have been given. They have taught me to love, to be kind, and to work hard. They remind me to stop and capture those special moments, with every breath I take.

After a long day and the last customer had gone, it was almost time to close, still a few things to finish up. Momma had headed home and left me to clean up. Broom in hand, I leaned on it, tilted my head back, and let out a long exhale.

The golden sun was setting in our little town. Another day was done. There is something to be said of daydreaming. It makes the time go by a little faster. I paused in the center of the small but quaint dining area, gently but carefully sweeping up the last of the daily grime from the well-traveled wood floors. The light coming in through the windows was beautiful. It was shining and warm, reflecting on the top of the dining tables and chairs, showing the warmth of the wood and years of patrons that had come and gone, like bringing down the curtain on the last act of a play. I finished up and pushed in the last of the chairs and wiped down the counters. I noticed the sun was almost faded from view, so I took a long slow bow, like a star of the stage for that final act. Walking to the door, I turned and looked back into the darkened store, reflecting on the day.

I turned the closed sign over, and locked the doors to begin my short bike ride home. As I stepped out and locked the door, I was startled by the appearance of a beautiful and fragrant gardenia, with a hand attached to it, suddenly appearing before my eyes. A crooked, knowing smile crossed my lips. It was Luke.

Luke Bennett, he held my heart for some time now; and at that moment, he also was holding my favorite flower on the earth. He knew it all too well. We had gone through years of school and church. His family was one of the many in our community that all grew up together. Church picnics, banquets, birthdays, school dances—we see each other almost every day at someplace or another. The side effects of small-town life.

His blue eyes shined, and his beyond charming smile greeted me from under that ragged blue hat he wore all the time. I spun around, "Luke! What are you doing here so late?"

"I thought I would come see if you wanted a ride home." I hesitated, only because if my parents caught me alone with him, there would be another war, a little closer to home. Against my better judgement, my heart won. He grabbed my bike and my hand, and off we ran to where he parked his old truck around the corner. He was a little older than me, and I am sure a lot more experienced, from my understanding. I am not sure what drew me to him, like a moth to a flame, but that was exactly what it was like, like two magnets feet or inches away instantly attracted, locked together, impossible to separate. He opened my side of the truck door to let me in. He slung my bike into the bed of his truck. As I went to climb in, he grabbed me and kissed me. He held me so tight I barely managed to breathe.

He stepped back and grinned, and he ran around the truck and climbed in to take me home. I could not stop smiling, and my heart was racing—one, because if Momma or Pops, or our nosy neighbor Edith, saw us drive up, I shudder to think what would happen; two, because I couldn't believe this was happening. I often dreamt this, but here it was, actually happening. I pinched my arm to make sure I wasn't dreaming. You know how I do that sometimes (when he was around, there was no one else). I would rather it just be the two of us, driving around in his truck or sitting next to him in class or at lunch. We had been spending a lot of time together, learning more about each other. I wasn't totally sure how he felt, but I was a goner. He looked over at me with that charmed smile, I melted. I was still smiling from the kiss!

As we got closer to the house, I said, "We probably should stop a street over, and let me out. I can ride my bike from there in case, someone is outside, or my neighbor is scanning the area for the latest gossip." I'm not sure what I was afraid of.

He laughed and said, "Okay, I could take you home and explain to your folks I gave you a ride."

"No. That is okay, but thank you for the ride. I enjoyed it."

He asked, "What day do you graduate? I want to come to the graduation."

I said, "A week from today, at four o'clock at the school auditorium."

He smiled and said, "I will be there. Well, I guess I will pull over here and let you get home. I will see you next week, if not before."

"Thank you again." I jumped out of the truck, but so did he. He grabbed my bike and set it in front of me, leaning over for one last kiss. He was so sweet. I grabbed my bike, then turned to wave and took off riding toward the house, with my flower in my hair. As I reached the big tree in the backyard, I stopped, leaned my bike up against it, totally out of breath. I closed my eyes and replayed the whole thing in my mind.

Did that just happen? I could smell the sweet fragrance of the gardenia from my hair, which reminded me I needed to take it out before my parents questioned me. I stuck it in my dress pocket so I could sneak inside and keep it in one of my books in my room.

Got up the next morning, ready to go, I had a big evening planned. Momma said I could go to the fair that just came to town. I was going to meet Rebecca, then walk to meet with Luke, along with his friend that is interested in Rebecca, John Reynolds or JR, as his friends called him. JR was not from around here, but Luke worked with him. He had known him for a couple of years. He had moved in with Luke's family at one time for a couple of months, when JR's dad had gotten sick. They were almost like brothers. I met Rebecca at the pub, and we walked over to the fair. The guys were waiting on us. They bought all the tickets we would need. JR had gotten Rebecca a snow cone, and Luke had gotten me a swirled cotton candy. I loved how it melted in my mouth, and the blue raspberry flavor was so good. We rode the merry-go-round, the Tilt-A-Whirl. We played I think almost every game in the Midway. We walked by one of the game counters.

"Step right up," the manager shouted. "How about you, young man? Care to try your hand at our shooting gallery, win your girl a prize!"

Luke was reluctant, but then he said, "Why not?" He stepped up and picked up the riffle and aimed like he knew his way around a gun. After four shots, *ping, ping, ping, ping,* one right after the other he hit every target. He won!

After a small celebration, the man said, "Go ahead, pick a prize, little lady."

I saw a doll with red hair. "I'll take that one, the red-haired flapper doll."

"Good choice! Kind of looks like you!" We walked down the midway, hand in hand, enjoying the warm evening air. We came to the Ferris wheel. This would be our last ride of the evening. It was getting late. We waited in line, handed over our tickets, and slid in to enjoy the ride and the views. You could see all over town from way up there. The sun was almost completely set on the horizon. The sky was a beautiful orange and pink. We were way up there! I almost forgot while I was admiring the sky how high up we truly were. We stopped almost all the way at the top. I reached over and grabbed his arm and held on tight. He said, "Just hold on, I've got you."

While we sat there, waiting to move, or maybe to be rescued, I said, "Thank you for today. I had a great time."

He looked at me and said, "So did I. I wouldn't want to be anywhere else." It was getting dark, and the crowd was thinning out. I had told Momma we would be home before dark. So we said our goodbyes, and off Rebecca and I went. We talked and laughed all the way home. Rebecca was not that into JR, but he was nice enough, she said. We talked about moving to the city after graduation and getting jobs at the Naval yard or one of the shops there in Charleston. Our options could be endless. But wherever my path took me, I hoped it ended with Luke.

Chapter 2

Sunday morning

Momma gets up early and prepares a hot breakfast for us, and we all get ready to head to church. The smell of warm biscuits and country ham cooking glides up the stairs and wakes me from a deep sleep and a wonderful dream. My brother Michael and I hit the floor, running to see who will consume the first biscuit with Momma's warm peach preserves. We stumbled and fumbled down the hallway, Mickie trying to pull on his church pants and button his shirt and me trying to pull on my socks and shoes before hitting that top step. I elbowed him right before the stairs, and he falls into the wall and about takes out the entire, precisely placed family wall of photos! I hollered back, "Sorry! Not!" I skipped the first couple of stairs, grabbed the railing, and slid down the banister right into my pop's arms.

He looked like he was about to take me to the woodshed. "What in the world is all the racket? Where is your brother? We have to eat and then off to church!"

"Sorry, Pop. Mickie is putting the family back on the wall before Momma notices."

Pops, with a puzzled look, said, "What are you talking about. Go on to the kitchen, Kat." Well, that did not bode well for Michael, but I did enjoy the first warm buttery biscuit right from the bowl. They were always sitting on the table, wrapped in a tea towel to keep them warm. The table set, Momma picked some fresh gardenia from the bush outside. It made the whole kitchen fill with that heavenly scent. Momma stood behind me and fixed my wild untamed hair while I ate.

Mickie came down, snuck around, and flicked my ear, as he walked by. I swung my arm wildly, trying to hit him, as he jumped to avoid the blow. "Now you too behave. It is the Lord's day!" Momma scolded.

Getting to church was a short ride, being in a small town, one of those where everyone knows everyone else and all their business to boot. It was a beautiful morning, so my brother and I, windows down, my arm hanging out, moving back and forth as if flying against the wind, bobbing and weaving as the air pushed back against my hand. Warm sun on my face, eyes closed, and my hair that Momma had painstakingly fixed earlier was being mangled by the warm breeze coming through the windows.

Once we arrived, I started looking for Rebecca. Let me tell you a little about Rebecca Thomas, my best friend in the whole world. I knew Rebecca basically all my life. We went through school together, every grade. So many adventures and memories, celebrations, and heartbreaks. We told each other everything, always there for each other, no matter what. Now coming to that age, where the fork in the road appears, forever friends, but our paths would possibly go in different directions. That made us both sad and a little afraid of having to deal with life events without each other. Rebecca graduated valedictorian of our class. I was less than an average Jane when it came to grades. She was popular and way prettier than me. She stood on the steps of the church, with several boys hanging around as usual, beautiful long blonde hair and always sharply dressed. I, on the other hand, appeared hopelessly basic—auburn hair, green eyes, and skin as pale as moonlight, my clothing decent but not as fancy as hers. We were so different, but none of that got in the way of our friendship. She spotted me and waved, walking away from her adoring fans just to come talk to me, and we scurried inside to find our seats.

Momma saved us a seat, and we hurried in because the music had already started. As we sang with our red, worn hymnals in hand, my mind started to wander, as it often did, thinking about graduation coming up and the party we planned to have at our house with family and a few close friends, but also hoping secretly that Luke would show up.

Gatherings at our house were always so much fun. We would usually have a low country boil spread, and everyone would bring some kind of southern dish that was a must at every get-together (creamed corn, peach cobbler, and, of course, fried chicken, because that was the easiest for the men to hold while tossing horseshoes in the yard). Portable poultry was a must-have. Then in the evening, we would either have fireworks and sparklers, or we would have a bonfire down on the beach. I imagined myself dressed in my graduation gown and the choker of pearls Grandma left me, hair in a popular style of the day and everyone applauding wildly as I came down the stairs from our front porch. I was waving my white gloved hand, like Queen Elizabeth did in the movie reels. This day has been a long time coming.

"Katie!" Momma whispered hastily.

I instantly dropped my hymnal. It made an echoing slap on the wood floor below. I closed my eyes, hoping to disappear, turning to see her sternly looking at me as she noticed my daydreaming. "Sorry, Momma," I mouthed. All eyes were glued on me all right, but they weren't applauding, just shaking their heads in a disapproving wag.

We all then sat down to listen to Rev. McClanahan as he delivered his sermon for the week. He started with one single word, *change*. "This word can invoke excitement, fear, or apprehension. We mostly crave normalcy. The repetitive comfort that the people we love, the things we have, will always be there. Sometimes the change is gradual, like waking up to a new gray hair, a change of the weather, your kids seem to grow inches overnight, the pregnant mother that appears to expand and grow leaps and bounds later in pregnancy, then more impacting changes like losing a job, relationships starting or ending, even the world around us changes values and priorities in the blink of an eye. We can go to bed one night and wake up to a completely different world as we knew it. It can make us fearful and feel abandoned, but we can hold on to that one constant. God never changes! The Bible says in Malachi 3:6, 'For I the Lord do not change; therefore you, O children of Jacob, are not consumed.' When things seem their darkest and hope lost, do not despair! God is our refuge and strength, a very present help in trouble. Therefore, we will not fear though the earth gives way, though the mountains be moved into the heart of the sea, though its waters roar and foam, though the mountains tremble at its swelling (Psalm 46:1–3).

"Things will always change, whether it is in ripples on a calm glassy pond or like waves crashing on the shore. Remember, no matter the changes we face ahead, He is with you. Look to Him, hold on to your faith. Now let us pray."

Of all the sermons I remember from Rev. McClanahan, this one stuck with me, not sure if it was because of the war or because I was getting ready to go through change with graduation; but growing up, this next chapter would be a big step. *Am I ready for this?* I pondered. *I will get through it. I'm not the first or the last person to walk this path.* Fear, I am sure, will be waiting on me and I had so many questions, but it was strangely exciting too. I had to have faith that everything would work out the way it was meant to be.

On our ride back home, we went through the center of town to make a stop at the drugstore. As we looked for a parking spot, I saw Luke's blue truck parked in front of Demetre grocery. He emerged from the store, arms full of groceries. He stopped as he reached the truck and noticed us passing. He smiled and moved the couple of fingers that were unoccupied to let me know he saw me. I smiled, ready to jump out the window, but waved slightly as to not to draw the attention of my brother. But my brother did see, and he poked me in my side. He made a surprised "better watch it" face. We parked across the street at the drugstore, and Pops went in. I watched for Luke's truck to go by. A few minutes later, I could hear that distinct engine coming down the street. As he passed, we locked eyes again. We smiled, and he drove on by.

I did not realize it, but I was hanging half out the window when Pops got back to the car. He said "Katie! What in heaven's name are you doing?"

"Sorry, I thought I saw Rebecca go by."

I ducked back in the car, and my brother said under his breath, "Sure you did, likely story. Someone is pining hard for Luke Bennett."

I reared back and smacked him on the arm. With my meanest glare, I whispered, "Shut up!" He laughed at me. Pops reached in the

17

back seat. We awaited a smack for fighting. But instead, we got the familiar "better stop it" glare and two grape Nehi he had bought for us as a treat! My favorite!

We arrived back home, and Momma started on lunch. We all grabbed a glass of iced tea and went to the porch where a nice breeze was blowing. Simple sandwiches were on the menu today. Momma wearily said she was going to lay down for her Sunday nap after she brought us our plates stacked with cold-cut sandwiches and her homemade million-dollar pickles. After eating, I cleaned up the kitchen for Momma, grabbed my bike, and headed a couple of streets over to Rebecca's house.

As I arrived at Rebecca's, I jumped off my bike, almost in mid-pedal. I ran up on the porch and knocked my special knock on the screen door. Her mom hollered from the kitchen, "Come on in, Katie!" She knew it was me. "Rebecca is upstairs in her room," she said. I ran upstairs, and there was Rebecca on her bed, looking at her movie magazines. She even got one from France! We loved looking at these for the latest fashions. This was one of our favorite pastimes. The clothes were so gorgeous, and the hairstyles were something to behold.

Rebecca always reminded me of Veronica Lake. Rita Hayworth is one of my favorites, she has red hair of course, and she was on the cover of the *Movie Stars Parade* magazine she just received. *Photoplay* and *Movie Star Parade* were a couple of our favorites, always containing great stories and lots of pictures. We finished looking at the magazines and started discussing what she planned on doing after graduation. She thought about going into nursing, wanting to help as much as she could, with the wounded coming back from the war. Rebecca said, "I think I heard Mom and Pop talking about moving. My grandmother is getting older, and not doing well. My mom wants to move closer to her to help."

I looked up caught off guard. "Where do they live?" I asked.

"Well, that is the bad news. They lived in Washington, DC."

"What!" I exclaimed.

"Yeah, a place in DC is opening up for Pop too for work. So it is pretty much a sure thing. Pop is leaving in two weeks, and we will be here for a while packing up and getting the house ready to sell."

I dropped my head. "Well, things I guess are changing a little faster than we had hoped."

Rebecca said, "Katie, the whole world is changing. It is scary. I want to go back to when there was no war, and everyone was home and happy. Just yesterday, a couple of houses down, a military car pulled up in front of the Stevens, and two men got out and walked to the house. They appeared in full military uniform. Mom and I, out in the yard, tended to some flower beds. Mom slowly rose and watched them drive by. She never looked at me but pointed to the house and told me to go inside. I said, 'But, Mom, we aren't done with the flowers.' She said insistently, 'Just go now!' As I got up to the stairs, I was startled by a scream coming from the house those men went to. It was Mrs. Stevens. She was screaming and crying and saying, 'No!' I was not sure why, but it scared me. I went inside and turned to see Mom run over to her house, waiting what seemed like forever for her to come back so I could ask what happened. Mom finally came back. She explained that Mrs. Stevens's older son that had enlisted, only deployed for a couple of months, had been killed in action. She explained, that is how some people find out about their loved ones when they pass."

"It feels like the world is falling apart. I am just not sure what will happen. But I know we will keep in touch and will always be friends. I promise." We hugged, both scared.

"Okay, so enough being sad for now. Maybe we can find something to help with at the local VFW. We can ask Mom. She is on a few local committees. I am not leaving tomorrow. We need to go over my speech. I want to see what you think. We also need to get ready for your party and pick a hairstyle out of one of my magazines!" Rebecca was always the strong one. She did not struggle with change, like I did. At least she never showed it. She was always my rock. What will I do when she leaves? I am glad I had Luke. He was strong and would be a good shoulder to lean on.

Chapter 3

"Momma!" I bellowed from the upstairs hallway. "Have you seen my pearl choker? You know the one Grandma gave me?"

Momma shouted back from the kitchen, "Look in your top drawer in the old jewelry box!" I scurried back to my room to search frantically, and there it was, the family jewelry box embossed with gold floral design, framing the light pink leather, with a gold latch on the front.

As I opened the box, it revealed treasures that had been left behind by so many before me. There were brooches and earrings and beautiful yet simple necklaces, all loved and cherished by those who had "moved on to the other side," as Momma always said.

There, under the memories, I found the pearls my grandmother and many mothers before her had worn for special occasions through the years.

Grandma had crossed over five years ago, but I still missed her and her hugs and singing in the kitchen, as she cooked and cleaned. She would sing hymns or songs from when she was a child. The beautiful sound had been silent for so long, but I can close my eyes and still imagine her standing in the kitchen, there in her church clothes, in house slippers, and her black apron with the brightly colored flowers on it, humming and singing, her salt and pepper hair styled with a single strip of toilet paper pinned around the back as she worked tirelessly, preparing a delicious meal. The table was set, everything in its place. The cake dish on the counter had a freshly baked, beautifully glazed Bundt cake. Lifting the top, you could smell the cinnamon, pecans, and that sweet glaze that, of course, I had to sneak a taste of from the glass plate. The heavenly scent of handmade baking biscuits filled the house, the baked steak, tenderized, and cooking in the iron skillet, splattering grease each time she lifted the lid to check the status. Then she would make the homemade gravy that went over the baked steak. Simple ingredients that, by themselves, no one in their right mind would eat are combined to make a salty velvet covering to the perfectly breaded and browned slice of cow. Of course, there were vegetables that got honorable mention. Oh! how I miss her.

Mother appeared in the door of my room, also in her slippers and apron, lovingly watching me go through the treasures and asks, "Did you find what you were looking for?" I smiled as tears ran down my face. "Yes, and much more. Thank you." Mother comes over to offer a hug. Hugs always make things better. "I do the same thing when I go through these memories."

"Honey, even though we have different memories, they are still so precious. Always hold on to them," Momma said.

We gathered all the treasures of the past and placed them back in the box. Graduation was in a few days, and I was just making sure I could find that choker. We then went down to the kitchen. Mother pulled out the old recipe box, and we made a batch of Grandma's biscuits. The house was filled with the warm buttery smell of rising biscuits in the oven. We gathered a couple of the family china plates, normally tucked away for holidays, and some preserves from the pantry in anticipation. Once done, we placed a decorative hand towel in a bowl and gingerly placed the hot biscuits in it to take to the old dining table. Momma and I sat there preparing our biscuits and sharing reflections we had of our childhood for what seemed like hours, laughing and crying and creating our own memories to carry on.

The days seemed to fly by. It was the day of graduation. I know I have always heard, when you get older, things seem to go by rapidly, just never thought it would happen this soon. The house was buzzing with activity. Decorations were going up. Food was being prepared and brought in with every soul that came through the screen door. That is the one thing that southern women have down to a science. It is preparing or offering food for every situation, or no situation at all. When you cross the threshold of a southern women's home, you should be prepared for a drink list and a small menu of delightful foods or desserts to be presented with a smile. Not ordering from said verbal menu is not an option. It can consist of leftovers or even a short trip to the store for that one item needed to complete the menu/delicacy requested. Or for the remainder of your visit, you will be subject to the repetition of these options, every hour, until something is consumed. Just know that when the food or drink is finally ingested, the joy and smile that you will see on the host's face makes it all worth it.

Mickie and Pop stayed busy, both outside decorating the porch that spans the full length of the house, you know, one of those porches that welcome you to stay awhile—rocking chairs and tables with glasses of freshly squeezed lemonade, ceiling fans spinning or wobbling in the heat of those hot humid summers. Mrs. Edith Gottleib lived next door. She was the nosy, no-filter neighbor, that on more than one occasion, had informed my parents of my and my brother's comings and goings. Actually, she informed every one of all comings and goings within earshot, or field of vision, from her kitchen window. "Yohoo!" she shrieked from across the yard, waving wildly with one hand and gripping her casserole dish in the other. She was peering over her horn-rimmed glasses, large, red apple earrings swinging from her long drooping earlobes from the weight of the said fruit, smiling from ear to ear. She got to the porch and stopped in her tracks to critique the decorations that were almost completed. "Patrick!" she hollered. "That sign is as crooked as a hound dog's leg!"

"Horse feathers," Pops whispered as he turned to look at her, smiled, waved, nodded, and went on to finish the task at hand. He learned long ago not to engage with her, and it would be much less painful. They finished up the decorations, and almost on cue, Mickie's friends came flying up the street, in their car, to whisk him away to no good, I am sure. He jumped down off the ladder and asked Dad if it was okay for him to go with them. He said, "Yes, but be at the auditorium by four for the graduation."

"Okay, Pops, will do!" They all jumped in and slowly backed out of the driveway. Then down at the corner, they took off with a squeal of the tires. Pop stood there shaking his head, running his hand through his black curly hair and a slight smile on his face.

Pops was a thoughtful man. He had quite the childhood. I sat with him that afternoon after setting up all the decorations. We sat under the beautiful Magnolia, in the front yard. He was feeling nostalgic. He talked more that day than any day I ever remember, like he needed to get something off his chest. He began telling me about when he was a boy. His father, my gramps, was a sailor and had been in WW1. He came home after the war and went straight to work as soon as he was able, back on the sea as a fisherman. Pops said he seemed almost possessed by the sea. He was not at ease unless he was on the water. If he was not on the water, he was sitting on the porch or on the beach, looking out at the horizon, almost like he was looking for something lost in the waters. Pops also mentioned he remembered he had a pocket watch on a chain that he carried everywhere with him. Grandma had given it to him before he left for war. It was one of his most prized possessions. It was lost in one of the battles at Gallipoli. Gramps did not talk about the war much, but he had written Grandma to let her know he was okay but had lost the watch. He had lost so much more. Most of his friends were killed in the blast that hit the ship. Grandma was just happy he was okay and coming home. He was discharged for his injuries. When he returned, it took a while for him to recover. Grandma tried to care for him as much as she could and take care of Pop, the house, and the pub. They needed help. A few friends and neighbors came to help. The ladies circle from church would come a couple times a week to help with meals and with some housework. But Gramps was not easygoing. So he ran off a few of the church patrons that came to help.

They needed someone that would come and stay there at the house and could put up with "Old Ironside" which is what all the caretakers nicknamed him. Momma decided it was time to call in the big guns, the only thing that could get through to "Old Ironsides"— Aunt Maggie.

Chapter 4

Enter Aunt Maggie, my pop's older sister, independent and resource-ful. She had Irish red hair and porcelain skin just like me! But she was a beauty. She lived in a B&B, in Isle of Palm. She employed a small staff that worked for her. She asked them to manage the bed and breakfast while she was away for those couple of months. She needed to help my grandma with the house, the pub, and my then much younger pops.

Aunt Mags had a mysterious past I was interested to learn more about. When we go to visit her, it's like a dream! The house is a mansion. The rooms all have different themes and are immaculately decorated with such detail. The gardens around the house seem to go on forever, flowers and plants of every variety. She owned one of those greenhouses where we would go and play in the dirt and help with tending to her plants when we visited.

Pops began to tell me about the day "Lifeboat Maggie" arrived to rescue them in their time of need. "We never noticed how she arrived. We just heard a knock at the door." She stood there, dressed to the 9s." That triggered my wild imagination. I could picture her standing in her finest frock, short hair style of the day, with a smart but elegant hat, with suitcases piled to her side. Pops said she walked in, and, of course, expected him to grab all her luggage. He took it all to her room upstairs. She greeted him with a kiss on the forehead and a hand to the hair, just to get a rise out of him. Sibling love, I know it well.

Among her many talents, besides horticulture and decorating, she was a good cook. She would prepare at least one thing we had never experienced. She said, "It awakens the senses and soul, to all the possibilities, when trying something new." It could be a new hairdo or an exhilarating car ride or something as simple as a light and creamy dessert laden with coffee and spirits." When she spoke, my mind would wander. I would get lost deep in my daydreaming world with all the possible adventures running through my head. See, she did it again, and she is not even here! I hope she shows up for graduation. She said she would be here, with bells on.

Pops continued to talk while I daydreamed, and I picked back up where he walked in to the kitchen while she was preparing dinner. Momma headed to the pub, tending to business. "Tonight," Aunt Mags said, "we are having an Italian feast, time we have something other than seafood in this house." She asked Pops to run and gather different things like tomatoes from the garden and pots and pans from the pantry. She even brought some fresh herbs straight from her gardens. Earlier she made a fresh loaf of bread and picked up a box of spaghetti noodles from the grocery. She put them on to boil. Then she started to prepare the never-before-experienced dessert, a thing she called, Tiramisu. This was also a classic Italian dish. She was going whole hog on this tasty adventure. My father vividly recounted every detail, like he was in that same trance I found myself in, when I was with her, like he was seeing it all again for the first time.

He said, "First, she placed the little white cakes and cream in layers. Then she pulled out the coffee and a small silver flask she tucked in her apron pocket. She mixed the two liquids and poured them carefully over each cake, making sure to cover each one. She layered the cream, then more cakes and more cream. Next came lots of whipped topping." Pops licked the spoons from the bowls. Removing her apron, she placed it on the hook by the door in the kitchen. They finished getting dinner ready. Momma came home, and they all sat down to eat. Then came dessert. He said it was the best thing he had ever tasted. He also said he kept thinking about that concoction she poured from the silver flask in her apron.

While the adults were all on the front porch, having evening coffee, he snuck back in the kitchen to find the flask. Pulling out the magic elixir, he ran out the back door, pausing for a moment behind the shed to inspect the contents—hooch, as some would call it, the secret ingredient. He ran down the street to where his friends were gathered, at one of the water inlets with a small fire going. He pulled out the flask, and they all took a few snorts.

After the festivities, he wandered home, dancing and singing to himself. He began his quiet entry into the backyard under the weeping willow, hoping to go up the back stairs undetected. Needless to say, when he got right to the tree, Aunt Mags stepped out of the dark, into the light that shone from the kitchen window. "Patty! What are you up to?" Pops said. He jumped five feet in the air it seemed.

"She scared the liver out of me! I was a little buzzed, but I sobered up a bit to find her waiting for me under that tree, in the dark." Aunt Mags enjoyed her last drag of the evening, away from the house where she spent most of her time these days. She was taking care of Pops and Grandpa and tending to the house chores. She happened to have two cups of coffee out there with her just by chance. She said, "You best stay here and drink some wits about you before you go in the house." She put out the last of her cigarette on the tree and drew her cup to her mouth. A slight grin came across her face, like she planned the whole thing. "Take time to learn from and enjoy these moments," Aunt Mags said.

After that night, he never looked at her the same way. She was not just his older, smarter, annoying big sister but a friend for life. He chuckled and shook his head. "Good ole Mags."

"Well, enough of this nonsense. We best be getting ready for graduation and all the festivities!" Pop said.

I jumped up with a grin, bent down to give Pops a kiss on the cheek. He grabbed my hand and said, "I love you to the moon and back, Katie girl." He said it in such a way I could feel it all around me like a hug. "Cherish these moments. Remember them always."

"I love you too, Pops," I said quickly. I jumped up and ran to the house to change. I passed Momma as I ran up to the porch she was headed out to where Pops was still under the tree. I looked back outside before I went to my room and there they stood, arm in arm, looking out over the dunes. That is one of those images that stay with you.

Chapter 5

I got to my room totally out of breath. Momma had ironed my dress and laid it on my bed, along with all the accessories, shoes, and with Grandma's pearl choker placed perfectly at the top. My graduation gown was hanging on the large armoire in my room. The sun was coming in the windows, just right, to shine on the choker and the graduation robe. My radio was playing Glenn Miller's "String of Pearls." It was like Grandma was there, acknowledging her approval of my choices and my success in this chapter of my life. I always looked for little signs like that when I had any doubts or fears in a moment. Suddenly, I heard something hit the window, like a bird pecking. I turned to look and nothing. I walked to the window to look out, and to my surprise, Luke was hanging precariously from the rose lattice that was attached to the house leading to my window. He was throwing little pebbles so not to make too much noise. I threw up the window. "What are you doing! You are going to break your neck!"

"Nah, I am okay, it's sturdy." He reached behind him and pulled out a small bunch of gardenias tied with twine. Handing them to me, he smiled. "I wanted to give you these, on your special day." He reached the window, grabbing the window sill and lifting his arms up to brace himself. He said, "You look beautiful in the evening light. I also wanted to tell you I am really falling for you. I have been, for a while now. I just hope I don't fall out of this window." He looked down to get his footing.

I said, "Just a second," ran to my door, and closed and locked it. Back to the window I ran and pulled him in. "I am falling for you too!" He wrapped his arms around me. We kissed. I heard rustling downstairs, so I knew everyone was coming to get ready. "You have to go now!" I whispered.

He did not want to leave, but he understood. He said, "I will see you at the graduation." I smiled, holding his face in my hands, memorizing his beautiful blue eyes for just a moment, my sweet Luke. I kissed him one more time as he went out the window. I watched nervously as he climbed down. He was almost to the bottom and jumped off. Looking up, he smiled and ran. I waved as he got in his truck parked on the street. The whole thing was like a movie. But the feeling was very real. I wanted to remember how I felt, right then, forever.

Then a knock at my bedroom door and someone was trying to open the door. I heard a slight ringing noise. Puzzled, I suddenly remembered, *Oh no, it's locked!* I hid my flowers in the armoire so I did not have to explain. I walked to the door, looking around to make sure no evidence was left, and I opened the door.

There she stood, Aunt Maggie! "How's my girl?" as she grabbed me up.

"Aunt Mags! I am so glad you are here!"

"I told you I would be, with bells on." She literally had bells on her charm bracelet that she jingled with the flip of her wrist. She looked beautiful! Her auburn hair stylishly coifed. Her dark green dress was simple, with a tie at the neck, made of the same dress material, short sleeves, pleats just above the waist, with a flat panel below, with kitten heel t-strap pumps. The makeup was light, but she had beautiful red lipstick to set off the whole look, quite a sight to behold. "Well, young lady, let's get you dressed! You have a date with destiny." I looked up at her a little stunned. She grinned at me with those red lips. How long had she been outside my door? Had she heard Luke and I? You remember Pop's story; she had a way of knowing things.

We finished getting ready, and I asked Pops if I could go ahead and ride with Aunt Mags. She had a new Green Pontiac, so shiny you could see your reflection in it, like a mirror! We rode through town to the school auditorium. Aunt Mags was something, with the windows partially down, sunglasses on just so, she had even purchased me a pair. People stopped on the street to turn and watch us go by, not many new fancy cars like this in our small town. I felt like I had my very own parade! Arriving at the auditorium, I started looking for Rebecca. I found her, and we squealed when we spotted each other. She had met Aunt Mags before, so she was greeted with a big hug too.

Over the loud speaker, they said, "Would all students gather backstage for pre-ceremony preparations." We all lined up in alphabetical order. Funny how you start with learning the alphabet, then you end with needing to know how to use it. As we lined up, all the girls were in their white dresses and robes, the boys in their shirts and ties and blue robes. Rebecca was preoccupied with her note cards, learning her speech. I was daydreaming again, wondering if Luke had shown up yet. I also wondered, if Aunt Mags had heard us in my room. Would she tell anyone? I had put one of the gardenia Luke gave me in my pocket. I could smell it, like a sweet perfume. The party would be right after all this formality. I was anxious, nervous, excited, worried, I might fall on the steps in front of everyone.

They handed us all programs, as we went back stage. I opened it to see my name and the order of the ceremony. Uh, where is my name? Why is my name not in the program?? I began to feel panicked. Did I fail, and they forgot to tell me? This is a nightmare come true, like standing in front of a crowd, in your dreams, to give a speech and realizing you are standing there in your underwear. I got the attention of one of the teachers back stage with us. I handed her the program, and she said it had to be a typo. Rebecca saw me crying and came over to where I was. She asked, "What happened?" I showed her the program. She hugged me and said, "I am sure it was an error. They will get it corrected." She went to the school secretary, and they checked the records. I did pass. They typed up a special program, just for me, so I would have one with my name. They apologized and stayed with me till I calmed down.

We walked out, in single file, and went to our predetermined seats. As I walked, I looked for my family and where they were sitting. Then I started looking for Luke. There he was, standing in the very back of the auditorium, up against the wall, scanning the line looking for me. Once we located each other, we smiled, and he winked. He looked so handsome. He was standing with his hands in his pockets. He had his dress shirt and sport jacket on and a nice pair of pants. I had not seen him look that nice in a while. After some introductions and Rebecca's speech, which she delivered like a pro, the parade of graduates began. We all walked, one by one, up to the stage, shaking the hands of several teachers, counselors, and the principal, before we were handed the first page of our new chapter in life. They came to my name, Katherine Anne O'Leary. It was a moment of fear and relief, knowing this chapter of my life was closing and a new one beginning. But the evening was young. What a roller-coaster day of emotions it had been. Little did I know, there was a tunnel on the tracks ahead.

Chapter 6

"That screen door has never been opened and closed so many times in its life! I think the hinges may come off!" Momma exclaimed. Friends and neighbors began to gather, all bringing a dish covered in mystery, only to be revealed later, with everything ready for the taking. Momma had Pops set up the tables in the shade of the porch. Everyone could file through and then head out to the trees for glorious shade from the evening sun. Momma asked us to spread out quilts and a few folding chairs for those who couldn't make the painful journey to sit on the ground. Pops gathered some wood for a bonfire later down on the beach. We all had sparklers and a few fireworks left from last year. We ran through the yard, on the sand dunes while the sun faded, a beautiful sight. Momma made my favorite, hummingbird cake. We left it inside in Grandma's covered cake dish, until time to eat it, no need to let that pretty white icing melt off in this heat. We sat down to enjoy a big glass of sweet tea after some games and a three-legged race. Of course, Rebecca and I won.

Aunt Mags was preparing to head home but wanted to give me my gift. She handed me the wrapped box. Inside was a bracelet with a single charm, a gardenia flower, also a journal with a pressed gardenia in the first page. She said I was to fill both gifts with beautiful memories so I would never forget. She said her goodbyes to everyone. Then she said, "Walk with me." I walked with her to her car. She smiled and hugged me. She said, "I am very proud of you." Then she moved in to whisper something to me, "Make sure you write down everything, even your dreams and those moments only you will remember."

She grinned and winked at me. She had been at my door when Luke was in my room. "I knew it!" Just as she went to get in her car, she turned back and said, "Guard your heart too. Things don't always go as planned. Expect the unexpected." I would not understand that whole conversation till many years later. Looking back, she was so right. We hugged, and she asked me to come stay with her in the fall for a few weeks. I was already packing in my mind and ready to go.

Everything calmed down, and everyone continued stuffing their faces with that wonderful food. We heard a car, come flyin' up the street. It was my brother and his buddies, they're back. They definitely made an entrance. All of them came walking down the hill after they filled their plates to overflowing. My brother, still standing, leaning against the tree, suddenly piped up and said, "Well, I enlisted today!" There was an instant quiet that came over the chatty bunch. My momma was clearly horrified. I thought she was going to burst. But she stood up, looked blankly in the distance and calmly walked in the house. My heart sank a little. My pops walked over to my brother, patted him on the back, and said, "Well, if that is what you feel you need to do, God speed, son." He walked over to the reverend said something quietly to him, and they began walking slowly to the house. Everyone resumed their chatter but nervously. I knew this was not going to be the wonderful evening I imagined it would be. I know it's selfish of me, but why couldn't he wait until after the party?! I am not sure if it's a boy thing, but he always seemed to enjoy in some way bringing shock and awe to our house, much to my parents' chagrin.

For example, once, he and his friends convinced Momma that they wanted to fix cookies for the bake sale at school on Monday. She looked at them like they had two heads, but she knew she didn't have time to do it herself. So she reluctantly left them to do the damage. She was rushing to get to the women's quilting club, so she told them to go ahead but clean up when they finished. "I do not want to come home to a wrecked kitchen."

Well, story goes that they used one of Momma's famous chocolate chip recipes. Those would sell the best. They were sure of it, but they decided to add a special ingredient. They finished with the baking. They smelled heavenly, filling the house with that warm chocolate scent. My pop came home and said, "What smells so good?" smiling with anticipation when he entered the kitchen, thinking Momma made them.

To his surprise, Mickie and a few of his buddies were washing dishes and cleaning up the mess. They all turned and looked, as if they'd been caught red-handed. Mickie said, "Hey, Dad, just making some of Mom's Cookies for a bake sale at school."

Pops looked at them suspiciously. "You all make sure this kitchen is spotless!"

"Yes, sir!" They chimed in unison. He turned with his pipe to go back to the porch. *What are they up to?* he thought to himself. The boys wrapped the cookies, piled them on a plate, and sat them on the counter to take to school Monday, then headed out the back door on their next mission.

A little later, Pop came back in to inspect the cleanup. "They did a decent job." He said to himself, shaking his head in approval. He looked to the end of the counter and saw the fresh warm cookies and thought, *They won't miss just a couple.* So he grabbed them, with some milk, and back out to the porch to wait for Momma to get home. After he consumed the delicious cookies, a short time passed, and he felt a small twinge in his stomach, then a gurgle. He sniffed the milk. It had that almost sour smell, but he drank it anyway. *You can't eat cookies without milk!* he thought to himself. Rubbing his stomach, he said, "Oh, I might regret that milk later."

Momma finally came home and was pleasantly surprised to find the kitchen as she left it. She started dinner, and we all enjoyed a nice quiet evening. Momma played a couple of songs on the piano, which set in the living room. When she played, we could sit on the porch and enjoy it from out there. Pop commented to Mickie, "I took a couple of cookies, and they were really good, almost like Mom's cookies!" Mickie's eyes looked like they would pop out of his head. "Why do you look so surprised?" Dad asked.

"Oh, no reason, glad you liked them. I think I will head to bed now. I've got to get to school early tomorrow to hand in my cookies."

"Okay, goodnight, son."

All of the sudden, in the middle of the night, there came a loud retching noise, seemingly from the hallway! Momma was hollering, "Get to the bathroom! Not on the floor! Not on the floor!"

We jumped out of bed to see what was happening. Dad was trying to get to the bathroom in the dark and trying not to vomit. I heard him say, "It is coming out the other end too! Are you trying to kill me? What did we eat?"

Momma said, "We are all fine! It seems to just be you! We all ate the same thing." Pops moaned and heaved what seemed like an hour. Mickie slithered suspiciously back to his room and closed the door. Mom stayed in there with Dad for a while until the attack slowed down. She went down to get him some water and saw something shiny, like a wrapper on the floor. She picked it up and discovered it was an Ex-Lax wrapper. Horrified, she put two and two together and decided not to tell Patrick tonight but wait till morning. They had enough excitement for one night.

At first light, Pop rose early like he always did. He was downstairs having coffee with Momma at the dining table. Mickie had just come down the stairs and was going to bypass them both by going out the front door. But Pops heard him and asked him to come to the kitchen. They sent me off to the bus stop. He was held to face the judgement. The story goes that Pops was eerily calm, like a snake you sneak up on and expect it to strike any second. Oddly, he did not strike. Either Momma talked him out of the whippin', or it was because every ounce of energy he possessed had gone down the toilet a few hours earlier. But he said he would have a "just punishment." It would just take some arranging. He said, "You will just have to wait for the final verdict."

Mickie would say later, "That was almost worse than goin' ahead and getting the painful whippin' I usually got."

Pops said, "You go on to school. We will talk later." He had to walk that morning. Well, come to find out, Pops did have a just punishment. There was a nursing home nearby for veterans, and he had a buddy who ran the place. He had my brother volunteer for a month, helping with janitorial services free of charge.

He learned some valuable lessons from that experience. He met some elderly men that were widowed and lived there full-time. Some they called short timers. They were recovering from a surgery or procedure until they were well enough to go home. One of the men he met, named Hank, was in the Great War. Boy, he told some stories. Some that would make you blush and others that would bring a tear to your eye. He went through so much. They all did. I decided one day, on a weekend, to tag along with Mickie and just go meet some of these characters he spoke of so fondly. Mickie really seemed to change, for the better, once he started working there part-time for his penance to Pops and the cookie debacle. He actually stayed on just so he could stay in touch with these men he now looked up to.

We walked in the door to a large common room. There were some men walking around, some in wheelchairs, others sitting at tables and playing games, some just sitting, staring out the big picture windows. Mickie said, "Let me introduce you to Hank." We walked over to a gentleman with all white hair, dress pants and dress shirt, no tie, and nice leather house slippers. He had stunning crystal blue eyes. He looked like what Cary Grant would look like when he gets older. Mickie introduced us, and then he went to work. "Hey, Hank," my brother said. "This is my kid sister, Katie. She wanted to come hang out for a couple of hours. She wanted to meet you."

Hank smiled, "Well, it is nice to finally meet you, Katie. Your brother speaks fondly of you." I quickly turned to look at Mickie. He rolled his eyes and went on his way. I wasn't sure if he was pulling my leg, but that was nice to know, if it was true. I sat with Hank for an hour. He told me he was a captain in the war and all about his men. He could recall most all of them. I guess when you go through something like that, it leaves a deep impression. He said, most of them were good guys. They had some bad apples, but they had their reasons. "People that come into your life, good and bad, are either a lesson or a blessin'." I learned a lot from Hank that day. I would return many times and see him and meet others, who all imparted some wisdom to me that I still carry with me. My brother really grew that summer, not only as a man but from a mischievous young man to an honorable and respected man in our town and in my eyes.

35

Chapter 7

People began to leave. The party was officially over.

Momma had gone to lay down, too much stress for one day. Everyone felt a little awkward after my brother's untimely announcement. So Momma's friends cleaned up and put away the food. Pop, my brother, and his friends all cleaned up the yard and took down the decorations. I asked them to leave the lanterns in the tree out front. It was so pretty at night to sit out there, under that big tree, with those lights giving off a soft glow. I decided to go for a walk on the beach. As I crossed the dunes in my bare feet, the cool sand felt so good between my toes. There was an old drift log that was just a little down the beach. I put on my charm bracelet and brought my journal along to write down the events of the day, so many to capture on these crisp new pages.

As I walked, I looked off at the horizon. The sun would be down soon. I decided just to walk a ways, then go back to the house and write in my room. As I walked down the beach, I noticed a figure walking toward me. I looked down and started looking for shells. The water gently lapping at my feet, it felt like bath water. I really wished we could have spent more time at the party. A bonfire and some songs would have been really fitting for the end of this day. As I looked up again, the figure was much closer. To my surprise, it was Luke! He said he thought that the party would have moved to the beach by now, and he could mingle in with the guests and find me. He wanted to talk to me alone. We met almost right at the old log. I sat down, and he sat beside me and took my hand. The sky was becoming that deep dark blue, with not a cloud in it. The stars were becoming brighter as the sun faded away. There was only a half moon which was perfect for lighting and viewing the stars. Luke said, "Which one do you like?"

I looked at him, with a puzzled look. "What?"

"Which star do you like? Which one would you pick if you had your choice of any of them?"

"Well, um, let me look a minute." I gazed from one side of the horizon to the other and looked for the brightest and biggest one. "That one there. It almost seems like it is twinkling? I like that one."

Luke said, "Okay, that one belongs to us. Our star connects us. No matter where we are or what we are doing, if we can find that star in the sky, you will know I am with you. Just look for it, and you will find me."

I looked at him and laughed, "You sound like you are going somewhere? Are you leaving?" I searched his face for reassurance of a no. My smile started to fade.

Luke looked at me for what seemed like forever, not with his usual smile but like he was memorizing my face. "I need to tell you something." He said it with a shake in his voice, not of fear but of sadness.

"You are scaring me. What is wrong? Have I done something? Did I say something wrong?"

I exclaimed. He grabbed both my hands to calm me down. Then he said, "I enlisted."

I stood up and started saying, "No, no, don't say that. You can't go! You can't leave now. I want to be with you! I can't be with you if they ship you off to God knows where." I started pacing, panicking, looking for words to change his mind to make this go away. *This cannot be happening. First, my brother and his friends, now Luke? Rebecca was moving to DC.* It seemed like my whole world was going away. "How long will you be gone? When did you do this? Let someone else go." I realized in that moment what I said. I was being selfish, wishing someone else would go in his place. I could tell he was calm and had been thinking about it for a while. He had remained on the log, sitting there waiting for me to finish processing it all, being totally silent and still. I could tell he was resolute in his decision. He wasn't asking for permission. He was a couple of years older than me. He had been working for a while, and a few of his buddies had already been sent overseas. He stood and walked over to me. Tears streaming down my cheeks, he stands in front of me, searching my eyes for understanding and support, wiping my tears with his fingers.

He says, "I know. I know it is going to be hard. I want to be with you too. I promise I will be careful and try my best to come back to you." Tears welled up in his eyes. He knew in his heart he might not be able to keep that promise, and so did I. He took me in his arms, held me tight, no music, just the waves crashing, the stars and the moonlight softly shining, as we swayed to comfort each other all alone on the soft sand. I wanted time to stop. I wanted to stay in this moment for as long as I could. I wanted to keep him here with me, and safe. But I knew his mind was made up. I had to let him go, at least for a while. He said, "I promise to write when I can. Send me pictures so I can keep you close. Remember our star. That will keep us connected." He stepped back and wiped the tears from my cheeks. "Always remember, I love you." He pulled me close.

"I love you too, Luke," I whispered with all the strength I had left. I reluctantly said I needed to get back home. It was late. He said he would stand there and watch me until I was back to my neighborhood to make sure I got back safe. As I walked away and the further we got from each other, I could still feel that pull, just like those magnets drawn inexplicably together, even with the distance. I looked back to see him standing there on the beach with the beautiful star filled sky behind him. No matter what happened, I will never forget that evening. I had a feeling my aunt's gifts were going to fill up fast. He was my first love.

I woke up the next morning, a little numb, so much to process, so much to prepare for. As much as I wanted time to stop, or at least stay there long enough to process and accept what was coming, but alas, that is not how life works. It keeps moving forward, and I would have to learn to move with it. This is the part of growing up. That pretty much never stops. Once you cross that line from graduation, you are thrown right into adulthood, starting with, "What is next? How do I transition from a carefree teenager to making my own decisions that will affect the rest of my life?" There really needs to be a warning label or a guide book for this part!

I only had a few weeks left to work in the Pub. Then I would be going to Aunt Mags to spend a month with her at the B&B. At least, there was that to look forward to. In the meantime, more change would be coming, no doubt.

Needless to say, I spent most evenings with Rebecca and/or Luke, trying to soak up as many memories with them as I possibly could. We went to movies and going-away parties for some of our friends who had enlisted. Rebecca's birthday was coming up, and it was a movie-star theme party. It would be the party of the year.

A few days passed and I spent this day with Rebecca and her mom packing up the dining room. They had so many dishes, serving trays, glasses, and punch bowls. I had never seen so much serving ware in one place, except at the pub. Ours were not this fancy at the pub. I think they could have had a party and hosted the entire neighborhood. They loved to entertain, and often did. Her dad worked for some military company out of Charleston. They had many holiday parties and summer soirées, ladies in fancy dresses, men in suits, or casual attire if they were headed to the beach, for part of the entertainment. I went to a couple of their parties during the holidays. It was like a runway show of the latest fashions. Rebecca and I loved seeing it all and critiquing each one on "Who wore it better?" especially if more than one guest came in the same dress. That was the BEST!

"So, Katie, what are your plans now that graduation is over?" Rebecca's mom asked.

"Well, I am still working at the pub most days, and in about a week, I will be headed to my Aunt Mags to stay with her for a few weeks. It will give me a little time to figure out what I really want to do."

"That is good you have her, and that time to consider your options," Mrs. Thomas said. "Has Rebecca told you her plans yet? She has a great opportunity to volunteer for a while at the hospital, near where we will be living. Then she can decide if nursing is what she really wants to do. I think it's very admirable that she wants to help with all the boys that will be coming home." She said while beaming a smile in Rebecca's direction. Clearly, she was proud.

Rebecca was smiling, but it seemed a little forced. Rebecca said, "Mom, can we take a break, maybe go get a soda?"

"Sure, honey. Take your time. We are almost done here, and the truck will be coming to put these boxes, in storage soon. You two have a good time."

Rebecca and I took our bikes and headed into town to the drugstore. It was a beautiful late summer evening. Soon the weather would be cooler. Our bike riding days together were numbered. We arrived at the drugstore, and they have a small diner that was a favorite local hangout for us and a lot of our friends.

Walking in, the soda fountain was in the front of the store. They had the stools that lined the counters. They were chrome, and they almost blinded you with their reflection as you walked in. The soda jerks were busy making the drinks and placing the short orders for the kitchen to fill. They had a small food menu. Our favorite was to get chocolate malts and share a plate of fries. This combination, while sitting in our favorite booth, made for a perfect place to work out all of the world's problems. We sat down, placed our order, and got down to the business at hand. Rebecca started, "Okay, so I have been thinking about you and Luke."

I said, "What about it?"

She started, "Well, you don't know how long he will be gone. You are young, with your whole life ahead of you. Yes, I sound like my mother. You are about to go away for at least a month to your Aunt's. Who knows what will happen, or who you might meet there?"

I looked at her with quizzical brow. "Why would I even think about that? I am totally falling for him!" How could she even think that? She knows how I feel.

Rebecca said, "Think about it, honestly. You are almost twenty. He is a guy that will be alone and thousands of miles away. Do you want to keep singing, 'Don't sit under the apple tree, with anyone else but me,' for the next year, or longer? You are only dating. True, you may be falling for each other, but all that could change for either of you at any time." Rebecca had a gift. She dealt with change seemingly with ease and adapted with her surroundings like a chameleon. I sort of admired that. But could I train my heart and mind to think that way? I understand what she was trying to say. It is a form of self-preservation and sanity to cut it off before he leaves. It just never crossed my mind. But I also believed in true love. Maybe I was just fooling myself. I remember my aunt telling me, "Guard your heart." Could we make it through all that might happen in the next year, or two, and pick up where we left off? I would love to say yes! But that is not reality. I am the dreamer. She is the realist. That is why we were friends. We balanced each other out.

Our order arrived and we dove in. I took that opportunity to ask her, "Why the forced smile earlier with your mom?"

Rebecca rolled her eyes. "They think they have this all planned out just because I said I might want to go to nursing school." They pulled strings with their connections at the hospital before I even agreed. So now, I am kind of locked in, unless I can find something else I want to do before I have to start at the hospital. I also had been looking into the local shops to try and get a job there in a department store." Her face lit up. "They have some great stores there, and designers come to that area a lot to design for dignitaries. That would be so much fun! I have a lot of work to do when I get there, to make connections." I had no doubt she would find a way to do exactly what she wanted or even all she wanted. She could multitask like that.

"What about wanting to help the war effort?"

Rebecca said, "I am torn. Wanting to have fun and wanting to help the soldiers, there has got to be a way to do both. I will figure it out, just need to get there and make connections with the locals."

I said, "Sounds like you have it all figured out so far." Her confidence was contagious, at least in the moment. My follow through, with making decisions, was the challenge for me. We both gave each other something to think about. Rebecca said, "Okay, now we need to plan for my party!" It happens right before you leave to go to your aunt's house, so we need to get to work." So our conversation went from world changing to party planning in the bite of a fry and a slurp of a malt.

Chapter 8

Three days before the birthday party of the century. The dress I ordered from Sears and Roebuck has not come yet. I am starting to panic. Every day I hear the mailman, Mr. Henry. I run to the porch to be greeted with, "Nothing yet, Katie."

I may need to go to town to the Secondhand Rose Clothes Shoppe. Maybe some of the rich ladies in town turned in a beautiful dress they no longer wanted. This is the last resort. I decided to ride into town to see what they have in stock. As I went through town, my thoughts went to Luke. I had not seen him in over a week which had given me some time to think about what Rebecca had said. Between both of us working and helping Rebecca and her mom, it was becoming more difficult to find time to get together. He would be leaving soon, so maybe it was fate's way of saying it might be best to move on. When he gets back, we could see what might happen. I was so proud of myself. I might actually be getting this change thing under control. I just needed to arrange to have a talk with him before he leaves. *Maybe at the party? Rebecca had invited him. We would not be completely alone, so it would be easier, maybe? I am saying maybe, a lot. Okay, stop thinking, or you will talk yourself out of it.*

So I got to the store and parked my bike right outside the shop. I wandered inside and started looking through the racks of clothes. *Wow, there are some pretty things here.* The shop owner was Mary Vance, she has a big personality, blonde hair, ample chest, and very curvy. The shop had been a long-standing business here in town. Growing up in this area, she grew up very poor but made her own way. Known for her generosity, she would help anyone that was struggling to find a job or get experience. She would lend them clothing for interviews and would coach them. She had knowledge and experience on how to make a living as a woman in the South. She had married a wealthy widower in town, and a few years after they married, he passed. She had been the talk of the town for quite a while after that. But she began to redeem herself after she started sincerely helping others. Using his enormous wealth, she would help others go further in life, quite a lady. "Hey there, honey! How are you doin' today? What can we help you find? Miss Katie, my, you have grown so much since I last saw you. You are turning into a beautiful young lady."

"Hi, Mrs. Vance, thank you," I said, feeling my cheeks red with blush. "I am looking for a dress to wear to Rebecca's birthday party. It is a movie-star theme party, so I need something flirty and grown-up."

"Well, let me think. I do have a few things out here on the floor and a few in the back that just came in. Let me grab them. You head on into the dressing room, and I will bring them to you straight away."

Next thing I know, she was knocking on the wall and said, "Katie, I hung them all out here outside your dressing room. Feel free to come out and pick whatever you like." There is no one else here but us chickens, so take your time." I opened the curtain, and there were five dresses. Two were a shade of red I could never pull off with my transparent skin, another was yellow. I had never worn yellow before. Next was a cream color one, which might have made me appear to be invisible. Ha! Then there was a green one that looked a lot like the one my aunt had worn to the graduation. I decided to try the yellow and then the green. Mrs. Vance hollered in, "Now, you try one on, and come out here where we can take a good look." The yellow was nice. It really made my hair look deep auburn. I stepped out. "Oh my!" Mrs. Vance exclaimed. That is right pretty on you! Turn around, let's see the fit, very nice. Did you pick another?"

"Yes, ma'am, the green one."

She smiled. "Oh, you must try that one on."

"Okay," I said, turning to go back in to the dressing room. I walked in and grabbed that one and put it on. It was even better on than on the hanger. It was just like my aunt's. Wait, what is this in the pocket? A petal, a shriveled white petal. It was my aunt's dress! How did it get here? I walked out, and Mrs. Vance was standing there, smiling like a cat who ate a canary.

"How do you like that one?" she said.

"Well, I love it. This is the dress my aunt wore to my graduation."

"Yes, it is," Mrs. Vance said knowingly. "Your aunt always stops by here, on her way out of town, to drop off a few things she thinks we could use. She has been doing it for years. It helps so much, and she is so fashionable. I make back money on the things I donate. She is a blessing!"

I looked at myself in the mirror and smiled and said, "Yes, she truly is one of those blessings." I had found my dress and learned a little more about my mysterious Aunt Mags.

Aunt Mags had also left the shoes and bag she carried with the dress that day at graduation. Mrs. Vance told me to leave it with her, and she would take it in a little and have it ready for me in two days, perfect timing.

I stopped at the drugstore on the way home to see if I could find a red lipstick. I found the perfect shade, Chili Pepper Red. They rang me up at the register, and as I stepped out of the door, there was Luke. My heart dropped, and so did the bag I was carrying. I bent down to get it, and the lipstick rolled out, right toward Luke. He bent down to pick it up and said, "What do we have here? Here comes the blood to my face."

"Oh, just some lipstick I picked up for Rebecca's party."

"Chili Pepper Red, nice." He smiled. He handed it back to me. I crammed it back in the bag. "Oh yeah, that is in a couple of days. It should be a really good time. I hope to see you there," he said.

That was an odd thing to say, I thought to myself. Was this not the same guy that said he really liked me after climbing my trellis, just a couple of weeks ago? He was acting a little stand-offish? Had something changed his mind? "Yeah, I can't wait." I was finding it hard to hide my feelings, regarding how he was acting. He seemed preoccupied. He leaned over to kiss me on the cheek and said, "I have got to get going. I am picking up my dad's meds and have to get back to him. I will see you at the party."

"Okay, see you then." I said with questionable tone, wondering why he was acting like that. Well, this might make it easier to have the talk with him if he is still acting like this. Hmm. I got on my bike and rode home. I don't even remember the ride. I was still thinking about how he acted like nothing had even happened. Maybe this is what my aunt meant by things aren't always as they seem. Maybe she knew something I didn't.

I got home and decided to start dinner for Momma. I got out the roaster and put in the potatoes, carrots, and onions, a little water, and then the roast on top. I placed it in the oven. I knew it would be a while, so I grabbed one of the *Movie Star* magazines and went out to the porch to enjoy the afternoon sun. I needed to get some color on my pasty skin. I found a couple of hair styles I liked. I might try them out. So I dog-eared the pages and enjoyed my cold glass of sweet tea.

What is that smell? I thought to myself. Then suddenly I jumped up and realized I had fallen asleep, sitting there in the sun. And I could smell the roast, and it smelled way more than burnt. I ran inside, and the kitchen was filling with smoke. "No, no, no, no! Not the roast." I threw open the windows and the kitchen door. Then suddenly, I felt extreme pain as the heat from the oven touched my skin. Oh my dear lord! I am the same color the roast was before it was cooked! I am totally fried. How long had I been out there? Ow, ow, ow. What am I going to do? The party is in three days! Hopefully, it will be better, but I probably will be peeling like a lizard. This day started out so perfect. It has gone downhill since then. They say an idle mind is the devil's playground. I think I was on his playground a little too long! Ouch.

Mrs. Gottlieb suddenly showed up with a big bucket of water. "Where is the fire? What's on fire? Get out of the way. I got it, Katie. Don't worry!" She throws the entire bucket of water on the smoking roast.

"Mrs. Gottlieb, nothing is on fire. I just burned the roast."

She looked at me, up and down in horror. "Oh, honey, looks like you burnt way more than the roast." She said in disbelief. "You come with me, and I will help you with that burn. I know you have that big party coming up." How does she know about the party? I walked slowly, and painfully, in tears to her house next door.

"I have this cream. I picked it up while in Atlantic City at the beach one year when I got sunburned. It smells strong, but it really helps." She proceeded to pull out this big, blue jar full of a white cream that kind of burned my nose when I smelled it. She smeared it all over my face, arms, and legs. My only saving grace was I didn't have my bathing suit on.

"I didn't realize, I fell asleep," I said, with tears in my eyes.

Mrs. Gottleib said, "I saw you sitting out there when I went to visit my mother, but when I came back, and you were still out there, with smoke rolling out of the back of the house. I knew something was wrong. I found my fire bucket and came running." I started laughing just then, thinking about her running in the back door with that bucket. All while, I was still crying and covered from head to toe in white cream.

She started to laugh too now that everything was okay. "I am sorry, I am a mess. I am not navigating this trying to be an adult thing very well yet."

She said, "Honey, believe me, I am way older than you, and I still don't do well at being an adult. It is a lifelong process. Don't be too hard on yourself, and just learn from your mistakes the first time so you don't get burnt again, literally, and figuratively speaking." We were both laughing then, and I was still crying while she tried to comfort me. I had her pegged wrong this whole time. She really became a dear friend.

Chapter 9

I had a secret. Well, it was not really a secret to everyone, but I loved to sing. I was in glee club in school. I probably got it from Momma. She would play the piano, and I would sing along on occasion. I heard about them, needing entertainment, down at the VFW for a couple of the dinners they had, so I would go there and sing a few songs for the old guys. They loved it. I had no grand aspirations. I just enjoyed singing to small crowds and at home with my radio.

Well, Rebecca's mom had asked me to sing a couple of songs at her birthday. She had hired a band to play for the party and wanted a couple of Rebecca's favorite songs performed. Who better to do it than her best friend? I was nervous and had been practicing with the band a little. I knew the songs well, so it was just getting the timing down. I think we were ready. Time to go pick up my dress. My painful sunburn, thanks to Mrs. Gottleib, had calmed down in the past couple of days, ode to that smelly, creamy concoction. I biked into town to grab my dress, and Mrs. Vance was so excited. "Have a wonderful time." She said she wished to be young again. She smiled thoughtfully and handed me the perfectly pressed dress, and I was on my way.

I got home and hung it on my armoire door, shoes laid out, stockings draped over the dress. I took a nice long bath and washed my hair, put on my big fluffy robe and slippers, grabbed my magazines, and plopped on the bed. I began looking at my dog-eared pages to see which hairstyle I would like to try. I finally decided on one and got to work. It was a little updo, so I could wear the last of the gardenias that were blooming on the bush outside in my hair. Momma came up to check on my progress and to help with the finishing touches. I was ready.

She said, "Are you nervous?"

I looked at her and said, "Yeah, a little, but I am only doing two songs, so it won't take long."

She hugged my shoulders, and while we both were looking in the mirror, she said, "You will do great."

"I will just pretend I am performing in Rebecca's room, like I did often with the radio," I replied. Momma ran down just before I left for the party and picked the biggest and best gardenias she could find and lined them in a row in the back of my hair. She secured them with I think every Bobby pin we had in the house. They may take root.

I put on my lipstick, stood up, and said, "Okay, how do I look?"

"Wow!" Momma said, "You are a beauty to behold! An Irish princess!" I rolled my eyes. Of course she would say that. She said, "Take a look for yourself." She opened the armoire door. There was a full-length mirror. She guided me over in front of the mirror. With raised eyebrows, I hardly recognized myself. As I stood there looking, Momma said, "Don't forget this." She grabbed my arm and put on my charm bracelet. Oh, yeah! I noticed another charm was dangling. It was a musical note. Momma said, "It's a little late, but it's a graduation present from your dad and I. We love you and are very proud of you!"

"Thank you. I love it!" We gently hugged so I would not get wrinkled, and off we went. She drove me over a little early so I could do sound checks with the band. The band sounded great. Rebecca was being distracted by her dad, away from the house, so it could all be set up in their grand backyard. It was beautiful. Once the sun started going down, there would be twinkle lights. They had been hanging in the trees. She was turning twenty, so they were pullin' out all the stops, beautiful pink flower arrangements on every table, white table clothes draped and pressed. Four people to a table was all set for a dinner that was catered. You would think she was getting married. That was just how they did things. I am just glad I got to enjoy it with her. I would be leaving soon to go to my aunt's. Luckily, it would be before they moved. Maybe it would not be as hard. Who knows when I would see her again? So many changes.

The party was starting. Everyone was wandering in. It was like a who's who. They had a red carpet, coming from the side of the house to the backyard. Everyone walked in, oohed and ahhed, as the band played popular songs we all knew and loved. There was a big opening in the center of the tables for dancing. There was lots of dancing. Rebecca finally showed up with her dad. He had bought her a car. She would need it when they moved, and she needed to drive around our small town, for practice, before going to the big city. As she stepped out of her car, flash bulbs were flashing. She looked like Veronica Lake. I knew she would! Her pretty blonde hair wore down, with the wave curls she was known for. The guys fell over each other to escort her in. It was comical. She came over to the main table, where we were sitting, smiling from ear to ear. This definitely was her day! She would never forget it, I am sure! It was so much fun, dancing and laughing, having the time of our lives!

It was time for me to sing. Rebecca looked at me when I stood up. "Where you goin'?" she asked.

"You'll see, you better appreciate this," I threatened. I got up and sang the first song, the name of the song was "At Last." This would be the hardest, but the band was so good no one would even notice me. Rebecca's mom and dad noticed I was nervous, so when the music started, they got up to start the dancing. Everyone joined in. It was a welcome distraction. To my delight, everyone applauded and seemed to enjoy it. Once it was over, there was a brief pause while the band was setting up for the next song. I got a drink, and a deep breath, now that was over. This next song was slow and more laid back. I decided to say something to Rebecca. I grabbed the mic and said, "I wanted to wish my best friend a wonderful birthday. We have been through everything together, and I wanted her to know how much she means to me by doing the one thing that is hard for me to do, perform in front of everyone. This is my present to you! Even though we are taking different paths, you will always be my best friend. Happy birthday!" Everyone clapped, and Rebecca was actually wiping away tears. She never cries.

My next song started, and I see Luke walk in from the back of the yard. The sun was going down, but the closer he got, I started getting that feeling again. The band had to play the intro twice to get my attention. It was "I'll Remember You." Doris Day's version was my favorite, so I tried to do it like she would. The words were kind of appropriate for this moment, seeing Luke. He walked slowly, with his hands in his pockets, all the way across the yard and leaned up against a tree. He looked up and noticed, it was me singing. He smiled and listened intently. After the song was over, I walked over to where he stood. He looked so great. He reached out to hug me. "That was beautiful. I am glad you decided to let other people hear your voice."

"Well, this is not a habit I am forming. I just did it, as a present for Rebecca," I said.

"It was great for you to do it anyway," he said.

"Thanks, finding it hard to take a compliment.

He said, "You look incredible too! I almost didn't recognize you. I see you wore the lipstick you bought that day from the drugstore."

I looked up and smiled. "Yep. That's the one." I needed to have the talk. All this stuff he was saying was making it harder by the moment. I needed to say what I planned and do it quick before my heart took over. "Luke, we need to talk honestly."

He said, "Yeah, I agree." We walked toward the back of the yard, overlooking the beach.

I started, "You are leaving. Who knows if or when you will be back. We have to be realistic, and I have to get my teenage brain out of the clouds. I do have feelings for you, strong feelings, but we are young, and both about to venture out into a world neither of us have ever encountered. I would like to think we will wind up together, but we cannot guarantee that will happen. So I think we need to put things on hold until you get back. Then we can see how the stars align."

Luke had been looking down at the ground most of the time. I wondered what he was thinking. He looked up at me with under-standing eyes and a slight smile. "You have been thinking the same thing as me."

"We can still write and keep in touch, can't we? You are my link to home. We still have our star too. By the way, I got you something," he said, remembering suddenly. He reached in his pocket and pulled out a box. "Go ahead open it." I had a look of shock and reached for it.

As I opened it, a smile crossed my face and brought a tear to my eye. It was a star charm for my bracelet. "Oh, Luke, I love it! Thank you!"

He helped me put it on and then said, "I have to report to basic day after tomorrow." I looked up quickly. Fear gripped me. He was looking down again, hands in his pockets. He was scared, even if just a little, but still confident in his decision. "I will miss you," he whispered.

"I will miss you too, Luke." We hugged. He gave me one last long kiss. He asked if I would come to the bus depot to see him off. I said, "Of course, I would." His dad was too sick to go, and his mom had to stay with him. So I and a few friends would be the ones to see him off. I was not looking forward to this part. This was not just another fork in the road.

The party ended, and everyone was gone, but the caterers and the last of the band. Rebecca and I sat at the table, reflecting on the evening. I told her about my talk with Luke, and she said she knew it was hard but probably for the best. "Who knows? You could still wind up together when he gets back? Or you could find a new exciting love on the path you will be taking starting next week."

"I will miss you, Rebecca."

"I will miss you too, Katie."

"Okay, no more tears," Rebecca said. I am removing my shoes, they are killing me, to get comfortable. She leaned under the table and pulled out two glasses and a bottle. "Let's drink some of this champagne I found." She popped the top, filled our glasses, and said, "Here's to us and the adventures that lie ahead." We talked, laughed, and cried way into the early morning. Well, at least I cried.

Chapter 10

"Last call for Columbus, Georgia!" The bus driver called. The sun was just rising, and there's a chill in the air. I had my overcoat on and just reaching the bus terminal. I did not want to get there too early because being around him for more than a few minutes proved to be fatal for me and my heart. But I was almost too late! I jumped off my bike and ran inside. There he was, standing there with his back to me, talking to some of our friends, giving hugs and handshakes to everyone. Someone saw me and pointed. Luke turned around and walked quickly toward me. He grabbed me up and said, "I was afraid you wouldn't show."

"I told you I would be here. I am not over you, Luke, just trying to let go as best I know how. You are still right here." I pointed to my heart. "Please be careful and come back."

He hugged me again. He whispered to me, "I will always love you. You are my reason for fighting to come back." I had brought him a picture to keep with him, something to comfort him if he began missing home."

I asked him to "please write, and let me know you are okay."

"Final call, ALL ABOARD!" the bus driver bellowed, echoing through the whole terminal. He looked at me one last time with tears in his eyes. He kissed me like he never kissed me before. He stepped back, looked at me one last time, grabbed his duffel bag, and disappeared into the bus.

I looked for him in the windows but could not find him. All I could do was wave blindly as they drove away. My heart ached. I did not get to tell him I loved him too. I said to myself, "I love you too. I love you too. Please come back." I sat on the bench outside the bus station, buried my face in my hands, and just broke down.

Suddenly, there was a hand on my shoulder. I looked up. It was my brother. He was leaving on the next bus. Mom and Dad were just inside. He said, "Wow, you really do have it bad for Luke. I will keep an eye out for him while I am over there." Somehow that was such a relief even though odds were they may never see each other.

"Thanks, Mickie. You be careful too! We love you. We need you here. You are my big brother."

"Yeah, I love you too, Katie," he said solemnly. Here came the next bus. Momma and Pops joined us outside. Momma was a mess. She would never be okay with this. Pops had his arm around her, more to hold her up than anything. I walked over and stood in front of them. Momma had a tight grip on my arm, like she was holding on to me by her last thread. Pops was being strong for both of us right now. Mickie hugged us all. We had to make Momma let go of him, and he jumped on the bus and got to a window so she could see him. She was fighting back the hysteria she felt until we got home. You could see it in her eyes and sense it all around her. Luckily, my aunt would be here later to stay overnight. Then we would be headed back to her house for a few weeks. The bus pulled away, and Momma would not move till the bus was out of sight. We got back to the house, and Pops helped Momma upstairs. And then he called Doc over to see if he could give Momma something to calm her down.

Rebecca was next to go after I left, but our goodbyes would be tomorrow. I could not take any more today. We had closed the pub for a few days to get acclimated to the changes. Aunt Mags arrived a couple of hours later, knowing she would need to manage the meals and chores until Momma could get back on her feet. I helped her with the chores. It was a welcomed distraction. Washing the clothes, hanging them on the line outside, Momma liked them best that way. I dusted the house and swept the front porch and fixed a fresh pitcher of iced tea. Aunt Mags fixed dinner, and we set the table. Momma managed to come down for dinner. Very little was said, but it was delicious.

Everyone turned in early exhausted from the day. I went to my room, closed the door, and noticed something sitting on the sill just outside my window. It was a note, with a yellow ribbon wrapped around it. The ribbon was lodged under the window. It was from Luke. He must have put it there before he left. I sat on my bed, holding it in my hands debating whether to open it or not. I finally got the courage to do it. It simply said, "I'll remember you." That was the song I sang at Rebecca's party. I had my hair in a pony and wore that ribbon that night and on days I was especially missing him. I still have that ribbon and note in my journal to this day.

Chapter 11

"It was the best of times. It was the worst of times." Mr. Dickens truer words have never been spoken. That whole quote is so true in my life right now. All these goodbyes and the new adventures ahead, I was not sure how to navigate all of this and all of these feelings I had. It was all happening so fast. Momma seemed a little better today. Not sure if it was all the sleep she had, but she was up early fixing a big breakfast with Aunt Mags. The house smelled so good, made me think of Mickie, racing him down the stairs to get that first biscuit. Seeing him wipe out the family picture wall made me chuckle recalling it all. It seemed so long ago. So much had happened since then, life-changing things. I was preparing to go downstairs and eat and then a little later, finish packing and head over to Rebecca's. I sat down at my mirror to fix my hair and readjusted my yellow ribbon. We were saying goodbye there at her house on the way out of town. They were all packed up and heading to a hotel for the next few days before they signed the papers on the sale of the house and headed North.

I bounded down the stairs, and Pops was there to greet me at the bottom. "Good morning, Katie." He reached out for a hug.

"Good morning, Pops. How is Momma?" I questioned. Pops looked at me, eyebrows raised but not a word was spoken. I guess that was a hint, not sure what I was walking into.

I walked in the kitchen, and Momma and Aunt Mags were working away. Momma was humming and seemed to have a whole orchestra playing in her mind, clad in her house slippers and apron and hair in a messy bun on her head. Aunt Mags looked at me with a reassuring grin. I know I had a totally puzzled look on my face. I quickly became aware and snapped out of it. "Mornin', Momma!" I said happily.

"Mornin', Katie!" she said with a slight slur and smile. Uh oh, it seems Aunt Mags had brought her magic flask and slipped my Momma a little home remedy for despair. This mixed with whatever med Doc gave her had resulted in a blissfully unaware Momma for now.

Aunt Mags came toward me. She whispered, "I only gave her a little in her coffee." But Momma was not a frequent participant in consuming spirits. So this would be an interesting breakfast. I chuckled a little to myself. So did Aunt Mags as she started loading the table with the feast Momma was preparing. We all sat down to a table of bacon, Momma's coffee grounds gravy, biscuits that were bigger than I had ever seen them, freshly squeezed orange juice, scrambled and fried eggs, toast, and every type of jam and preserve that they could find in the pantry. They would have plenty of left overs for Pops to take with him to work.

Momma said, "Okay, does anyone need anything? Napkins, salt, pepper."

"No, Momma, I think everything is here. Come sit down."

"Where is Mickie? He should be down here by now?" Momma said, looking toward the stairs.

We all looked at each other, not sure what to say. Pops decided to change the subject. "Honey, I think I need some more coffee." She stood up to grab his cup and refill it immediately. I think after she said it, she realized what she said and remembered Mickie was gone. She appeared embarrassed and kind of teared up. We never spoke of her lapse again. Momma, over the next few months, would learn to deal with his absence for now. I called to check on her from Aunt Mags frequently. The afternoon passed quickly. It was time to head out to see Rebecca and then head North to Aunt Mags's house.

Pops loaded the last of the luggage in the car and came back inside to let us know it was all ready. Momma walked up to me and said, "I love you, honey. Have a wonderful time." She seemed okay with me leaving because she knew I would be with Aunt Mags but also that I was not too far away.

"I will be back, Momma. I love you too."

She said, "I know you will." Then she turned around and went back in the house. I looked at Pops concerned. He walked up and said, "Don't worry, honey. She will be okay. Her brother and sister are coming to visit. It will be a distraction, and they will help out. They called last night. I felt relieved."

"That is great. That makes me feel much better."

Aunt Mags said, "Let's get going so we can get home before dark." We got in the car and headed out. Pops waved and headed back in the house to check on Momma. Mrs. Gottlieb came out on the porch as we drove away to give us a wave goodbye.

Next up, saying so long to Rebecca. We pulled up in front of the house, and Rebecca was sitting on the porch. The movers were coming in and out of the house with boxes and the last of the furniture. Aunt Mags said, "I will wait here for you." She waved and smiled at Rebecca. I got out and walked up on the porch, looking up at the house we grew up in together and shared so many memories. It was kind of sad to think I would never go in it again. I am way too sentimental. Rebecca said, "Hey, you made it. We are leaving in about an hour."

"You know I am not good at this kind of thing."

"I got you a present. Hold on." She jumped up and came back with a box. It was so pretty.

I said embarrassed, "I am sorry I did not get you anything."

She said, "It is not big, just something to remember me by."

I opened the box. It was a bike charm. "Oh, Rebecca, I love it! Thank you. We will keep in touch. Just write me and send the letters to the house. I will be back in a month."

Rebecca said, "Yes, we definitely will write."

"You will always be my best friend." She was not much for hugs or crying, but both happened. Then it was time to go. I got back in the car and rolled down the window to wave until we were down the street and out of sight. Aunt Mags grabbed my hand while I quietly mourned yet another goodbye. At some point, I dozed off. I hoped this next chapter of life will not be filled with so much loss.

Chapter 12

"We are here, sleepy head," Aunt Mags said. She gently nudged me as we pulled in her driveway. I opened my eyes. There it stood in all its grandness, still as beautiful as I remember, trellises, with lots of ivy creeping on them. She had stunning zinnias, peony bushes, and wisteria all growing beside the house. Her gardens were amazing. All the shrubs are cut to a certain shape and size. Something was always blooming. She loved color, which was also true in the house. The main house was very neutral, but each room had its own theme. Traveling a lot before settling here, she used all the treasures she collected to decorate. She had a carriage house out back, with four separate doors. I had only seen the inside of one of them, the others locked up. I am sure there were many more things to discover.

She pulled into the garage. A car was parked outside, must have been a boarder. Someone was always coming or going since this was a B&B. Some stayed longer than others. She has some real stories to tell about each person that has ever registered at the old B&B. She always had a way of pulling out life stories from people when they lodged with her for any length of time. She told me to grab my bags and meet her in the kitchen. Then she would tell me which rooms I had to pick from.

I walked in the kitchen with all my luggage and dropped them at the door. I may have brought too much. I saw someone bend over, leaning into the refrigerator. "Miss Millie!" I said.

"Katie, is that you?" she said.

"Yes, ma'am!" I ran over to give her a big hug. Miss Millie had worked with Aunt Mags for years. She was such a help and a good cook, probably where Aunt Mags learned her skills. Miss Millie owned this grand house. Her and her husband bought it many years ago. After he passed, she was not able to care for the grand house by herself, so somehow my aunt and her came to an agreement. Aunt Mags purchased the house, but only if she stayed and helped her run the B&B. It was a win-win for everyone. Miss Millie loved the company of the boarders and was a social butterfly.

"Dinner will be a little later around six o'clock. You can help if you like, Katie."

"Miss Millie, I would love that. I have lots to learn!" She smiled and raised her eyebrows in agreement.

Aunt Mags came back in and said, "Okay, you can head upstairs. Any of the rooms to the right, at the top of the stairs, are available." Aunt Mags just kind of said in passing, seeming to be preoccupied in doing something else.

I grabbed my bag and headed up the grand staircase, still as grand and beautiful as I remembered. I got to the top, after lugging all my bags, collapsing under the weight of them and making a lot of noise. Every sound echoed in the big, grand staircase. Someone opened one of the suite doors just to the left of the stairs. A man emerged with hair disheveled and attired in full old-man pajamas. "Could you please be quiet! Some people are trying to sleep!"

I picked myself up and apologized, and he poked back in his room like a mole and slammed the door. "Note to self, be quiet and watch out for Grumps." He earned a nickname due to his pleasant attitude and attire. I wish Rebecca was here. She would appreciate this encounter, and we would have a good laugh. I found my room, decorated in all the décor from India. The colors were incredible. I had no idea what some items were. This would give my imagination and dreams food for thought. I put my things away and headed back down, quietly of course, to help with dinner. I had found a hat, or turban as I came to find out from Aunt Mags, and decided to wear it to help with dinner—guess I set the mood because they decided to make some traditional Indian dishes to break me in. Well, this would be a true adventure. They showed me the spices and let me smell and taste each one. We made a bread they called naan. We were all three, me, Miss Millie and Aunt Mags, dancing and singing in the kitchen, all around the large wood table. We drummed on the counter where they prepared all the ingredients. The smells were very strong, filling the kitchen.

A moment later, Grumps came downstairs, standing in the arched doorway, looking disgusted. He said, "What is that smell?"

Aunt Mags said, "Well, Mr. Livingston, tonight we are having Indian cuisine. It should be ready soon."

He snarled up his nose and said, "No, thanks. I am headed out, but thank you." He turned and left as quickly as he appeared.

Where was he going this late in the evening? Aunt Mags said that man is a mystery. "He is sometimes gone all night, then shows up in the morning, maybe grab some coffee, and then he disappears to his room, until time for him to leave again. I have only seen him out of his room a couple of times, but he spends it in the garden totally alone, or reading a book. He keeps to himself. I am sure he has a story, just not sure I will get to hear his." I looked toward where he had been standing, intrigued, sounds like a mystery that needs solving. Katherine O'Leary is on the case.

Dinner was served. Just the three of us, so we sat down. My aunt had brought some colorful scarves and candles and other décor to set up the scene for our epic meal. I had never had Indian food but was eager to try, smelled delicious. As we ate, the flavors tasted so good, but I began to sweat a bit. The spices were beginning to hit my virgin stomach that had up to that point, just had a steady diet of typical southern food, not that many strong spices used where I come from. The bread was very good and garlicky. It seemed to help, with a bit of the fire that had been lit in my gut. After dinner was adjourned, we cleaned up and gathered on the porch to observe the neighborhood happenings before retiring for the evening. I took a walk in the gardens and took my journal with me to record the events of the day. My bracelet had a bit of a jingle now, with all the charms I had collected so far. When I heard them, I would be reminded of everyone with each charm. As I sat writing, the sun was setting, so I headed back to my room. I fell asleep while writing midsentence.

Sometime early in the morning, my stomach started to cramp and rumble. "Oh no. I have got to get to the bathroom!" Now I know what Pops had gone through that time with my brother's "special" cookies.

I grabbed my slippers and ran with my hand on my mouth to the bathroom. I threw open the door, felt for the light, and switched it on with eyes closed, a voice from the bathtub shouted, "Get out! Occupied! Occupied!" Grumps was sitting in the tub in the dark. I had no time to explain. I ran to the toilet and vomited my adventurous dinner into the porcelain bowl. I barely made the target. Grumps jumped up, grabbed his towel, mumbled something under his breath, and stormed out dripping wet, from the bathroom into his room.

My aunt was alarmed by the ruckus and came running. "Are you okay? What happened?"

"I don't think dinner agreed with me. Neither does Grumps now. He was in the bathtub. I couldn't wait." Aunt Mags chuckled a bit while getting a wet rag to put on my neck and head. The meal continued to reappear for a short time, and she helped me back to bed. She brought me some water and stomach medicine and sat with me till I fell asleep. I lay on my soft pillow while she was rubbing my head with the cool cloth, I said, with all the energy I had left, "Maybe we should have started out with a little milder cuisine."

Aunt Mags said, "I am so sorry, just rest now. We will be easier on your next meal."

"Thank you," I said as I moaned and closed my eyes to sleep.

Chapter 13

There was a knock on the door. Was it morning already? Ugh, what a night. "Katie, are you still alive?" My aunt whispered through the door.

"Yes, I think so," I groaned. "What time is it?"

"Ten o'clock, time to rise and shine. I thought we might take a drive. We need to get you behind the wheel."

That woke me up. My eyes opened wide. "Really?" I said.

"Yes, it's time, my dear. I am not going to be your chauffeur forever. You wake up and come down for some toast. Something mild will be best." She chuckled as she walked away from the door.

I got up slowly and gathered my things and off to the bathroom. Caution gripped me as I approached the bathroom. "Oh, I better knock since some people don't use lights," I said under my breath, hoping Grumps somehow heard me. It was safe. No occupants.

I got ready and headed down to the kitchen. I had a couple of pieces of toast and a glass of water. That was all I could take. A few minutes later, we hear footsteps on the stairs. Uh oh. I thought to myself, *Heads down, and quiet till he leaves.* He walks into the room, in a dress shirt, nice pants, smart-looking shoes, and heads right for the coffee without even a glance. "Good morning," my Aunt Mags says.

"Morning," he says mid-sip. He grabs several spoons of sugar, but that was all. Pure black was what he preferred.

"We are headed out to learn how to drive today. This is my niece, Katie."

"Hey"—he looks my way—"Oh, yes, the intruder. By the way, a banana or applesauce might help with your gut."

I said, "Oh, thank you. Sorry about last night. It was dark, I had an emergency."

He interrupted, "I know." He rinsed his cup, set it in the sink, and turned to leave. "Have fun driving. Better late than never," he said under his breath. I thought to myself, *What a jerk.* I don't think I have ever encountered a more unpleasant human. What could he be doing with the schedule he keeps?

Aunt Mags said, "He told me he would not be here but a couple more days. Then he is moving on."

"Well, that will be nice. Then it will just be us till the next boarder."

"Yes, but that won't be for a few weeks. This is our slow season. Then you will be going home for the holidays. Your Momma will need you."

We headed out to drive around on some back roads. She had that beautiful car. I was so scared. She was very patient. We laughed, I cried, it was quite the experience. I got stuck on a hill. I had to pull the emergency brake and let her maneuver us out of that predicament. We drove for a couple of hours—parked, backed up, used the blinkers, all the things. Then she decided to let me drive home. Most of the road was a straight stretch. We took it slow, but we arrived safely. She had me just park in the driveway. "Not quite ready to pull into the garage," she said. We would do this every day for the next week. Then I took the written test and passed with flying colors. A few days later, I took the driving portion nervously and cautiously. I got through it and was prepared for the road. She still rode with me, if I needed to go anywhere. We drove into Charleston one weekend and walked around the shops and ate at McCrady's. I heard George Washington was a patron here on occasion!

Aunt Mags suggested I pick up some applications in the stores I thought I would like to work in. So I grabbed a few. Then we headed to the beach. I had not been to Sullivan's Island in a long time. It was my favorite place. Station 18 was my spot. We stopped on the way back to take in some sun and fresh air. My aunt had a friend near the where we were headed. We could change and grab some chairs. I brought my journal to write in and filled out my applications for employment. We had carried our chairs and umbrella out to enjoy the afternoon. I sat in the sun with plenty of lotion on this time. I also had a large brimmed hat and the sunglasses Aunt Mags had purchased for me a while back.

We talked on the way home. She said, "You know if you would like to work in Charleston, you could come stay with me as long as you like. You could work, make some money, then eventually rent your own place. Something to work toward, you need to start your own life."

I knew she was right. I was gaining more confidence with each experience I was having here. Getting a job and saving money would be the next step. I need to purchase a car too. "That sounds like a good idea. I will think about it." I said as I was thinking ahead. We arrived back home late in the evening, and Miss Millie had fixed some grilled cheese sandwiches and tomato bisque. Sitting at the table was Grumps. I guess it was his day off. We left early and were gone all day. He looked up startled and started wrapping up what was left of his sandwich and walked out the back door to the garden. "That was rude," I said.

Miss Millie said, "No, that is just him. We have learned, small talk is not his forte. He leaves day after tomorrow. According to what he paid today. He said that would be his last day here."

"Well, good riddance," I said as a matter of fact. We sat down and told Miss Millie about our day, and she told us about some jobs she used to do in Charleston. She said if I needed references, she would be happy to put in a good word. She had some connections. "Great!" I said. "Thank you!"

I decided to head out to the gardens after we finished our meal. The sun was almost down, the crickets and frogs were chirping, and the lighting is beautiful that time of day. I wandered in and found a plant I had never seen before, looks like an earring shaped like a heart, with a white bead dangling below. As I stooped down to observe it closer, I heard, "Dicentra."

I turned to look, and it is Grumps. "Pardon?" I said.

"That is the name of the plant, or the burning/bleeding heart, as it is commonly called."

"Oh, that makes sense. They are beautiful."

He says sadly, "They were my mother's favorite. They will be gone soon. When the weather gets cold, their season is over."

"Were her favorite?" I asked.

He looked down and said, "Yes, she passed a couple of years ago."

"I am so sorry, everything has its season."

"Yes, yes it does," he says thoughtfully. I could not help but notice his beautiful gray blue eyes and brown wavy hair. The sadness in his voice seemed to slip out without his noticing. I almost felt sorry for him. Then I reached to pull off a bloom. He snapped back into his Grumps persona. "What are you doing?" he scolded.

"You said it would be gone soon. I wanted a bloom to keep in my journal," I responded.

"It will be gone soon, not yet! Let it live its life out and go naturally," he said and walked away in disbelief. "You are a child. You don't understand," he whispered under his breath as he walked back to the house. *Sorry? Seems there may be more to that story*, I thought to myself.

The next day we did not see Grumps at all, not until late that evening. He left without any of us knowing. He did not return until wee hours of the morning. I heard the back door in the kitchen open and shut because I was still awake writing in my journal. I never heard him come up the stairs. It had been quite a while since I had heard anything, so I was afraid maybe it was someone unsavory wandering in. I snuck down the stairs. I looked in the kitchen. I saw his bag sitting in the floor, just outside the kitchen. I peeked around the wall. There in the front room was Grumps, sitting in the chair, elbow resting on the arm, with his hand holding his head, dress shirt sleeves rolled up, and he was slouched down in the chair about to slide out. At a closer look, his sleeves were covered in something red like it was stained or he had been painting. He looked so peaceful sleeping. He seemed very messy, like he had been in a fight or struggle. I saw a jacket hanging on the coatrack with sleeves appearing to be wet. I looked closer and noticed there was dripping on the floor. It was blood. Stepping back quickly, I was startled and tripped over the rug.

He looked up squinting, rubbing his eyes trying to focus. I ran up the stairs. He said, "Who is there!" I ran as fast as I could and got to my room and locked the door. I turned out my light and hid under the covers. Oh my god, had he killed someone? The hours he keeps, he could be a serial killer. I did not sleep at all that night. My mind was going nonstop. He would be gone tomorrow. Then maybe we would be safe. He appeared to have a short fuse, even possibly, a sharp knife.

I fell asleep at some point. I don't remember even drifting off. But the next day, he was gone. I guess he left in the middle night. I am glad, he was a very unnerving person. Hopefully he moves on to another state now that I had seen the evidence of whatever he was doing.

I wound up staying until late November with Aunt Mags and Miss Millie. The days were packed with so many wonderful memories, trips to the beach, picnics at a few of my aunt's friend's houses in Charleston Harbor. I met lots of girls my age. I made several new friends. Yes, I was introduced to a few nice guys too, nothing serious, just someone to date, for now. One of them I befriended, worked at one of the shops where I had turned in an application. She said when I was ready, she would put in a word for me. I was getting excited for this next adventure. We just had to get through the holidays, which may prove to be pretty lonely this year. I did miss Momma and Pops and looked forward to sleeping in my own bed. It was good to get away so I could think for a while and make plans for my future.

Chapter 14

The phone rang. I heard Aunt Mags answer. After talking for a little while, she came in and said, "Your Pops is on the phone."

I got up and ran to the phone. "Hey, Pops."

"Hi, honey, how are you doin'?"

"Good, I will be home in a couple of days," I said, kind of wondering why he called.

"Yes, it will be good to see you. I wanted to call and give you a heads up about your Momma. She lost a lot of weight, and she's kind of withdrawn. The Doc said she's not sick, just a bad case of depression. She is medicated, but she sleeps a lot. I think you comin' home will bring her right out of it. But I wanted to warn ya. Also, you got some mail here. Your dress that never showed up finally did, and you got a letter from Rebecca and Luke."

"I got letters! Okay, oh I can't wait to read them. I miss them so much. I have so much to tell them. Miss you too. Thanks, Pops. Give Momma my love. I will be home in a couple of days."

"Bye, honey," he said. He sounded so down. I had to go home.

One last party to go to before I leave. I have had so much fun and learned a lot. This was a military ball that my aunt was helping with, and I was invited by one of my friends to go. I had never been to one before. We headed to town to find dresses. We came home, and I started getting ready. Aunt Mags said she had a couple things to do, then she would be getting ready too. I just finished my bath and headed to my room. I heard something on the roof. What was that? I knew there was an attic but had not been up there in years. "Aunt Mags?" I yelled down the stairs.

Miss Millie said, "She's not down here, honey."

I decided to venture up the stairs to the attic. I slowly climbed and heard a radio. It wasn't playing music, more like a short wave, like my brother used to have. I got up to the top but saw nothing. I listened for where the sound came from. I saw a hatch door with a string hanging down. Slowly pulling on the string, there appeared a set of stairs. I climbed up, and there stood my aunt in a small room with a big window, binoculars and a large telescope, just a table with a radio and a chair. She looked back at me from her binoculars. "What are you doin' up here?" How did you find me?"

"I heard the radio and followed the sound."

"You cannot tell anyone about this," she said. I looked at her a little worried.

"What are you doing up here?" I asked emphatically. "Are you a spy?"

"No, silly. Well, not technically." My eyes widened, and my mind started wandering.

Aunt Mags said, "Get hold of yourself, girl. There are many of us that have volunteered to take shifts as plane spotters." As I got closer to the table, I saw a book called *The Plane Spotters Guide*, sitting there opened. She wasn't kidding. "We all take shifts, and if we see a plane, we have code words to call in that gives the plane description, the location, and the direction. I have radio connection. Some people use phones. It is a volunteer group of people that just want to help in the war effort. I watch for two hours. Then Miss Millie comes up for the second two." That explains why there are times during the day Miss Millie would not be around. I just thought she took a nap.

"Can I take a look?" I asked.

"Sure, good timing. One is coming over now. I will show you what to look for." She started asking me questions about the plane. She could identify it with just a few questions. "What about the direction?" Then she got on the mic and gave her code words to a male voice that responded, then silence. *Wow! This is so interesting*, I thought to myself, still trying to figure all this out. Aunt Mags said, "You go on, honey, and get ready. I will be down later. Just one more hour."

"Okay," I looked back at her as I climbed down stairs on the hatch, standing there in her dress and heels, doing her patriotic duty in silence, but what she was doing was important, quietly doing her part here in the states, watching the skies from our homes, people all over the US, on all coasts doing the same thing. The things you learn when you listen or watch closely can be amazing. I need to do more.

All ready to go—hair fixed, makeup done, dress on, and raring to dance. I grabbed my shoes and headed down the stairs. When I got to the bottom, I put my shoes on and looked up. There she stood in all her glory, Ms. USA, Aunt Mags. She wore a beautiful bright blue dress, hair looked perfect. She was something else. "Are we ready?" she said.

"Let's go," I chimed back. She said, "You look lovely, Katie. You will be like honey to those flies." She smiled with raised eyebrows.

We drove up the long driveway to where the party had started. Valets waited outside to take the cars and park them. We just walked in, like we owned the place. Everyone knew Aunt Mags. I don't think she ever met a stranger. She volunteered to help with the food and punch. She told me to go on in to the main hall where everyone was gathered and dancing with a big band. They sounded great, almost like Glenn Miller's band. So many people dancing and having a great time, I decided to grab a seat and just watch everyone. A couple of my friends came over and started talking when suddenly, from across the floor, I saw Grumps! Why was he here? Looking for a new victim? I moved over just a little so I could watch him without being seen. Dressed in full naval uniform, wow, he looked great. Who can say anyone in uniform looks bad? He held two glasses of punch and walked over to a pretty blonde in a red dress. She smiled, and he just casually handed her the drink, seemingly uninterested, just scanning the room while she chatted him up. I think I saw him roll his eyes a couple of times. He looked like he needed rescuing. I don't think I would be the welcomed sight he wished for though. Then my aunt probably spotted him at the punch bowl. She walked over his way and asked him to dance, known for not being shy. The incredulous look on the girl's face made me laugh out loud, totally disgusted with my aunt imposing on her territory. They danced a couple of dances. He looked relieved and seemed to enjoy himself. My aunt's charm and wit could talk the hind legs off an ass, a jackass that is, one of the other nicknames I gave him while he boarded at the B&B. Hopefully, he's not sizing her up to fit in his trunk. I am sure she could take him out if needed.

He left shortly after they danced. The party really started jumpin' the later it became. I think there may have been some liquid courage being added to the punch. I was asked to dance a few times and may have broken a shoe doing the Lindy, the perfect ending to my visit with my Aunt. I had grown up considerably and had a lot to think about when I got home to see what my next steps would be. After the New Year, hopefully things would get a little more normal so I could get back to planning my future. Maybe a big move loomed on the horizon.

We got home pretty late. We tried to be quiet, coming in the back door, but we laughed like two school girls that had been partying way too hard. I had not enjoyed myself like that since Rebecca's birthday. Sitting in the kitchen that night, after we changed into our pajamas, I learned so much more about Aunt Mags. She made us some exotic tea found on one of her many trips abroad. She fell in love with a diplomat when she was younger and ran off with him against her parents' advice, living a whole life in a short time. He, being a little older than her, like ten years older, she fell head over heels. To her delight, being with him included traveling, seeing places she never thought she would, all with the love of her life. She met some extraordinary people and saw things I will probably only see in my magazines and in movies. They were together for seven wonderful years. She said, "It was so short." But she regretted nothing and would do it all again. He passed suddenly while they vacationed in India. After my encounter with the Indian food, I could totally understand passing due to the food. Her heart was broken, and it took a long time to get to where she could at least be okay with it. She enjoyed all the fun, extravagance, and travel; but she could have loved him forever, even without all that. He left her everything he owned, including his fortune. He made sure to take care of her, even if he would not be there to do it himself.

This story sounded familiar. Those feelings, pushed back for a while, hidden, by all the new excitement, but hardly a day went by that I did not think of Luke. I could not wait till I got home to read the letters. I secretly hoped he thought of me too. Wanting to be strong and let him go, but I can still feel the pull, after all this time, and him so far away, living through God knows what. Like the tide, sometimes you just can't fight it. Only time would tell how our stories might end, but the one thing my aunt taught me, don't waste your life standing still. Enjoy every minute, savor the experiences, love someone with all your heart. It is always worth it.

Chapter 15

There is just something about an old diner—those leather seats, the shiny chrome on the stools and booths, the smell of fried food, even the cleaner the busboy just used to wipe down the booth you were seated in. As the waitress invites you to sit a spell and hands each person a plastic-covered menu with front and back pages and everyone orders a less than healthy meal, that will forever be etched in your memory. Rebecca and I loved to go to our local soda shop. Those were the best fries with lots of ketchup.

There was a nice diner on the drive back home. Aunt Mags and I decided to stop on the way while listening to the radio and singing along to every song. It was a pretty busy place since it was right by the highway. Truck drivers, weary from driving the long hours on the roads to earn a living, stopped to grab a bite. Families came in with their kids that won't stay in their seats. Needless to say, they did not stay long. Then there were some girls that came in laughing and having a good time. I had a flash of when Rebecca and I would go have our plate of fries and our malts. All of our friends would be there too. Aunt Mags said, "Where are you?"

"Oh sorry. I was just thinking back to when I was able to be with my friends before they all went away. I'm afraid the holidays are going to be so lonely. I miss Momma and Pops, but it is not going to be the same, almost dread going back. But I know I need to for Momma. I need to help her get up and moving again, fixing her some good food with the things I learned from you and Miss Millie. That will fatten her up. I wonder if Pops might have to sell the pub. I hope he does not think I can manage it. I don't want to stay there. I want to get out and experience life."

Aunt Mags looked at me. She said, "Katie, we all have different paths we have to take. Not all of them are free from briers and rocks. Some obstacles, we have to take on to move forward. Just don't lose sight of the beautiful beach ahead." I knew she was right, but that was not what I wanted to hear.

We finished up and headed back on the road. I was excited to get home but also apprehensive because I was not sure what to expect. We reached the city limits. Aunt Mags pulled over to let me drive the rest of the way. I got to drive into town. She had to drop off some of her clothes and shoes at the Second Hand Rose. We picked up a few things at the grocery, then headed home. Aunt Mags decided to stay overnight, to get me back into the groove and be there if I needed her. Pulling in the driveway, Pops was on the porch reading the paper. He heard the car and peaked over and saw me at the wheel. He folded it and placed it on the table beside him, sat his cup of tea on top and stood up a little surprised. "Katie, you are driving?"

I smiled so proud. "Yeah, Pops! Aunt Mags has been teaching me and letting me practice. I am getting more confident."

He looked at Aunt Mags. "Did she drive all the way here?"

"No, Patty. She is doing well but still supervised," she said, with one eyebrow raised.

Pops said, "You look so much older. You have sprouted a foot it seems?"

"It has not been that long," I said. He stepped in for a hug. I still had to get on my tiptoes to hug him, but not as much. Maybe I had gotten taller. I know I felt more grown-up inside, at least.

Mrs. Gottleib came out on her porch and hollered, "Hey, Katie! Welcome home," as she tended to the hundreds of plants she had on her porch. She would be taking them indoors soon, into her large sunroom, where she spent most of her time monitoring the neighborhood for the latest news of the day.

"Hey, Mrs. Gottleib!" I waved from the porch. I headed in the house.

Pops said, "Your package is on the hall table, with all of your mail as well."

"Thank you," I shouted back as I ran to the table.

73

I grabbed my stuff and ran up to Momma's room. I got to the top of the stairs and began to walk slowly so not to startle her. Standing at her door, there she sat quietly in her comfy floral chair, looking out the big picture window in their bedroom. Knocking on the door, I said, "Momma?"

"Katie? she replied. "Come in, sweetheart!" I walked over to her, and there she was, in her house coat and slippers. Her hair was grayer, and she was so thin. I tried not to look shocked. She looked at me and smiled and said "I am okay, just tired." I did not hide my shock well enough, I guess.

"Hey, I know. I understand." I tried to sound upbeat and not as concerned as I felt. Kneeling down beside her, with my package and letters, opening some of them with her might entertain her somehow. "Look, Momma, this is the dress I was supposed to wear at Rebecca's birthday."

"Oh yeah, how was that dear? Did you have fun?"

I looked at her confused because I had told her all about it when I got home from the party more than a month ago. She did not remember? I was not sure if I should read the letters. It might be too confusing. "Aunt Mags is here. Let's go down and see what she is fixing for dinner. Maybe we can help."

"Okay, that sounds nice," she replied.

We went down, and Momma seemed to liven up a bit with the activity happening in the kitchen. She did not help as much, but she did want a chair so she could sit close and observe when she got too tired to stand. Aunt Mags had bought several healthy vegetables and some fruits for a cobbler. We found the ice cream machine. Pops pulled it out and got it working. We added some fresh fruit to it for extra flavor. It was so good. It was a nice evening, so we all went outside to enjoy the cooler weather. And Momma seemed to be energized a bit, not sure if it was Aunt Mags cooking or if it was me being back home. At least I was home now. Maybe that would help her get back to normal as things can be, knowing your son is facing death on a daily basis.

After dinner, I went to my room. Everything was still in its place. I sat down on my bed and anxiously read the letters Rebecca and Luke had sent. Rebecca said that she had found her connections she needed to work in the department store, and she did work there a short time. Then she decided to enroll in nursing school. She said it was a whole other world there, and everyone did everything to advance the war effort. It was contagious. That is what helped her decide to do the nursing thing instead. She had met a few really great guys and had some good friends, but she missed spending time with me and hoped I was doing okay and had found some friends to fill the void she had left. She said she was sorry. After she left, she realized that I would be alone, with Luke leaving and her and my brother. That was a lot to deal with at one time. Her next letter was shorter just because she had already started school and was very busy. She told me some crazy stories about cadavers they worked on, also so many parties and practical jokes the students would play on each other. It sounds like she found her niche. I was happy for her but also a little jealous.

The letter from Luke seemed very lonely. He did meet a couple of guys that had grown up down here in South Carolina, so they had lots to talk about, made it a little less lonely knowing someone that understood where and what you were talking about, missing the same things, remembering places that you were familiar with too. He said he missed me and that he looked for our star in the night sky when they were out on patrol or bedded down for the evening. I finished his letter. I decided to take a walk on the beach. I grabbed my favorite blanket and headed out. Pops said, "Don't be gone long."

I said, "Okay." I jogged down the stairs into the yard. I had not been there since he left, somehow hoping I would see him there, even though I knew that was not possible. I came over the dunes, feeling that cool sand, hearing the waves, seeing the moon rising and the stars shining so bright. It was like the night knew I was coming and made itself as perfect as possible. The stars were so incredibly vivid. I looked to the right, and there, just down the beach was where we sat when he told me he was leaving. My heart felt so heavy. Those feelings came back. I decided to walk down and sit for a while. I reached the log and sat down, stretching out my feet, digging them into the sand, looking up to find our star. Closing my eyes, I pictured him walking down the beach toward me, hands in his pockets, white t-shirt on, with that blue ragged hat. He was looking down, as he was walking toward me slowly. It was like he was walking in place. He never got closer, but he was close enough for me to see him clearly in my mind. I could almost feel him all around me. His presence with me felt real. I did not want to open my eyes because that would mean he was not really here. After a few minutes, I snapped back into reality. It started to sprinkle rain, and I had to get back before I got drenched. When I looked up, the clouds had rolled in, and the stars were completely hidden. It was very strange.

After Aunt Mags left, Momma seemed to come out of her fog. Every day, she got a bit stronger. I had never seen her like that before. It gave me a new appreciation for motherhood and to not take her for granted. The thought of her not being around and giving up was impossible to imagine.

She actually started having me drive her to the pub a few days a week. She would work with the ladies they hired to help them learn the recipes she was famous for, wanting to keep them the same as long as they owned the pub. I had a good talk with her and Pops to let them know I did not want to manage the pub, and they understood. They had already started preparing a new staff after I left because they knew my heart was not in the business. They wanted me to do whatever I wanted to do. That had been their dream, and they had lived it. They said it was my turn to find mine. I was so glad they felt that way.

The holidays were not too bad. Momma's family came to visit. She was feeling much better for Thanksgiving and fixed a huge meal, even invited some neighbors and the reverend. She had gotten a couple of letters from my brother, which seemed to really light a fire in her. It was reassurance that he was okay. He had seen some heavy fighting but had come through, okay so far. Christmas came, and the town had a huge get-together in honor of those that were deployed. Momma got very involved and decorated the pub. There was a gathering in town, and the names of those deployed and serving were read aloud while we all lit candles. We lit the big tree and sang carols together. All the town being together seemed to comfort everyone. People brought food and had eggnog and punch. I hung with a few friends that I had not seen in a while. They had been away at school and came home for the holidays. I had been spending my days helping Momma and helping at the pub a few days a week just to make some money to get that car I would need to be able to work in Charleston. Overall, the holidays were good. With Momma doing better and the help they had hired would make it easier to leave after the holidays for work in the city. Time to start moving forward on my own path.

Chapter 16

"Katie, mail is here from Charleston," Pops bellowed up the stairs. I popped up, got dressed, and ran down stairs. I grabbed the letters off the table and started going through the mail. There were two responses. I had two interviews scheduled at the end of next week. This is so exciting! What will I wear? What do I say? I need references. Oh no. How am I gonna get there? I had some work to do.

I needed to run Momma into town to drop her off at the pub, and I headed to Second Hand Rose. I needed a dress, smart but stylish. Mrs. Vance would know what to do and be able to help me know what to expect in the interview. She coached many women and men who were entering the working world, her gift in life, a consultant for the future working person.

I walked into the store, and she welcomed me with open arms. She said, "You want to dress fit the type of job you are interviewing for. You want to look put together, polished, ready to go. You need to smile. People are much more receptive to a happy person than a frowning nervous Nellie. You want to be that way for any job. If you work in stock first, then work on the sales floor, you want to show the same attitude for either job. Both are equally important. If the stock girl does not do her job by making the merchandise presentable, and in the best condition, the sales person cannot do her job of making the customer fall in love with it, and ultimately take it home. You are a team when you work in a business. When you don't, you will not succeed. Now let's go over some questions they may ask in the interview. You want to keep your answers short and sincere. Be genuine, not fake. A lot of people, especially other ladies, can sense when you are not being genuine."

Mrs. Vance gave me a list of questions they might ask. She told me to take them home and write down my answers, then bring them back in a couple of days. "I will critique your answers and let you know if I have any suggestions. Now let's get to the necessary attire. I think there is a cute gray tweed peplum, two-piece suit that would be perfect, in the back, then a sensible pair of black heels and a choker of pearls."

"Oh no, I have the pearls!" I said. "My grandmother left me a pair of my very own. They give me confidence when I wear them."

"That is perfect," Mrs. Vance said. "Every girl needs a set of pearls that she can depend on. Let me get the suit, and you can try it on. And we will see what alterations need done."

I tried the suit on, it was perfect, just a little hem to get it the perfect length. "Thank you so much for your help. I can never repay you for all this valuable information."

Mrs. Vance looked at me and smiled. She said, "Katie, the way you repay me is going out and fulfilling your dream. Be happy. Share what you learn with other girls and ladies. A lot of women don't have the benefit of strong women to look up to. Having access to the knowledge and generosity you have here in this town is a blessing. You are a fortunate soul to have been given your special family and the friends that you gathered so far. I am excited to see where you go and what you do." I hugged her and headed out to pick up Momma.

After a successful day in town, Momma started dinner. I ran up to finish my letters to Rebecca and Luke. I had been back for several weeks and had only gotten one more letter from Luke. Rebecca sent a few since I was writing her back. I need to think about how I am going to get to the interviews. I need to talk to Aunt Mags. She did offer for me to stay there. Maybe I could borrow her car, or she could take me to the interviews. But then what if I get the job? How will I get to work? I may need to take her up on her offer. It makes sense. I could stay till I can get a roommate or find a room somewhere in town. My aunt does have connections.

I called her the next day. We discussed the logistics, and it really only made sense for me to move in with her for now. I could save money, be closer to work, and a little more independent. She agreed.

I decided to talk with Momma and Pops that evening. There was not much time to wait. The interview was scheduled at the end of next week.

We just sat down for dinner, discussed the events of the day. Momma had been at the pub, and Pops just got home from many hours of fishing. He brought in a good catch. They started training some new crew. Because he is getting to the age, he just wanted to manage from home, letting others do the hard work. He still loved the sea but began preparing to watch it from the porch. I started discussing the move and my interviews with them. Momma got quiet. Pops said he was not thrilled with me thinking of living on my own yet. I said, "That is down the road. I am not ready for that either, also needed to save for a car." They decided it probably would be the best solution for now. I then told them I would need to leave at the beginning of next week. Momma got up and started clearing the table. Pops looked at me with pursed lips and raised eyebrows. I knew she would not take it well, but the time was fast approaching. I got up and started helping. Pops decided he would be best served with his newspaper and iced tea on the porch. So he took his leave.

I walked up and placed the rest of the dishes gently in the sink. I grabbed Momma's hand and looked at her. "Momma, I will be okay. I am not that far away. I can come home once in a while. I know it bothers you, but I have to do this, want to do this. Please, I need you to be okay with it. I don't want you to be sad."

Momma looked at me with tears in her eyes. "I know, sweetheart, you are my last baby to leave the nest. I cannot promise not to be sad. But I can tell you I will be okay. Having support in place now, for when I feel down, and your father will be home more too. I just need to get used to the changes." I reminded her about that sermon that we heard at church. She said that the reverend spoke with her about that too, when she was getting counseling. "I want you to be happy and chase your dreams," she said. "I just wish your dreams lead you closer to home. It will be fine." We hugged and both cried. It is hard to leave but kind of exciting too at least for me, well, time to start packing.

The next few days I spent gathering and organizing everything I needed to take. I went out to the storage building, looking forward the extra suitcases we had, it's gonna take a few. I also needed to run down to the Second Hand Rose to pick up my suit. Pops actually said I could take the car. I was nervous and would be alone in the car, but I had driven quite a bit, so I will be fine. I thought to myself, *It should be fine. I will be fine. Okay, get hold of yourself, just jump already!*

He tossed me the keys and said, "Be careful."

"Of course, Pops," I said with confidence, pretty good acting job, if I do say so myself.

I sat in the car, started it up, turned on the radio low so I could hear but not get distracted. I put it in reverse and pulled out. Wow, my maiden voyage on my own. It was so liberating and scary. I got to the town city limits and knew to slow down. I coasted in at Mrs. Vance's. She was standing outside and saw me pull up in the parking space. "Well, look at you, driving all by yourself."

"Yes, I am. A little scary, but it was okay. I have to be ready to drive myself to work in Charleston if I get one of the jobs." She asked for my list of answers. Looking at them while I tried on the suit, a few minutes later, I emerged from the dressing room. Mrs. Vance said, "Now, there is a beautiful young lady." She mentioned I did very well on my answers, and she just had a couple of suggestions. I was proud, like I had just passed a big test. She wrapped everything up for me, and I was on my way. I gave her a big hug and thanked her again. "I will try my best to make you proud. I will try my best to share what you taught me, and I do plan on being happy. I will come see you the next time I am in town."

In the next couple of days, we heard an announcement that there would be gas rationing, and only public transportation would be used for traveling long distances for a while. So my plans were already getting shaken up, expect the unexpected. I decided to take the Greyhound to my aunt's house. This would be one of those rocks in the path my aunt spoke of.

Chapter 17

"Last call for boarding," the porter shouted. Here we were again, early in the morning, fog heavy, and that winter chill in the air.

Pops had pulled the car up front and unloaded my three suitcases. "I feel like I am forgetting something," I said.

"Well, if there is anything, we can mail it to you," Momma said. Pops grunted as he heaved the suitcases out of the trunk. "As heavy as these are, how could you have forgotten something?"

Momma laughed. "Now, Patty, a girl has to have everything she could need when she is traveling."

Pops looked at her. "Now, woman, how would you know? You are not a world traveler."

Momma looked at him. "I inherited all the travel books, and now I will have all of Katie's movie magazines to keep up with the latest and greatest." In all my thoughts about myself and what I was gonna do, I forgot that this will be the first time Momma and Pops will be alone, like they were, right after they got married, twenty-four years ago. They were acting like they were dating, Pops being playful poking at her and Momma, even though I know she was sad I was leaving, giggled like a schoolgirl. They will be just fine. It is like a second chance to be young and enjoy each other without kids around. You tend to forget they are not just your parents. They were boyfriend and girlfriend first, then husband and wife and then parents. It was so different to see them that way, another part of growing up, realizing your parents were once like you. They had dreams and fears and hopes just like I did. Pops would be home more and Momma just helping at the pub. They can enjoy their life now. Momma was involved in several church functions and Pops still helping on the docks, but not going out anymore. He knew Momma needed him home. After all, she is his first love, the sea in a distant second place.

I took my sweater from Momma, gave them both a long hug and a kiss on the cheek. I had never seen Pops cry, not even when Mickie left. But he had a tear in his eye after he hugged me tight. He was always so strong. I love them both so much. I climbed on the bus and found my seat by the window, wanting to be able to wave and see the town as I left.

Waving, I blew them a kiss, and we were off, watching as we passed the church, the drugstore, the Second Hand Rose. Mrs. Vance had put a sign in the window, "Good luck, Katie!" That made me smile. We passed by the school, and then after we got out of the city limits, we went past Luke's house. There was his old blue truck parked in the yard with a tarp over it, just waiting for him to return. I thought everyone was leaving me. But I just had not started my journey yet. Maybe I am the lucky one because I left last. It kind of makes it easier, knowing Luke is not there, and Rebecca has already moved. I hope Luke is okay. I haven't heard from him in quite some time, still continuing to write, hoping they are reaching him.

At some point, I fell asleep on the trip. There was no music, and there was one old guy that was snoring and a lady with a baby that was very fussy. We had a couple of stops on the way, so I would get out and walk and get a drink once we stopped.

The bus driver announced we would be stopping in about ten minutes. I woke up and fixed my hair and put on my sweater. As we drove along, I saw a girl walking, struggling with a suitcase, along the side of the road, dangerously close to the oncoming traffic. I wondered where she could be going. Once we got to the gas station, the driver said we would be there about fifteen minutes. I got out and went to the restroom and grabbed a drink. I sat out in front of the station, on the bench, and drank my grape Nehi. Looking around, I spotted that girl with the suitcase, approaching the station. She was covered with dirt and grime, from walking in the road. She looked so tired, staring and walking toward me. I thought I better move over so she can sit down. She reached me, dropped her bags, and plopped on the bench. She had been traveling quite a while from the looks of her. Her hands were red and swollen probably from carrying all that weight.

She bent over, with her head in her hands. I said, "Would you like a drink?"

"Yes, that would be lovely," she said. She had a strong English accent. "A glass of water would be wonderful."

I went inside and grabbed a cup with some water from the fountain. I took it to her, and she inhaled it and got a little choked. "Careful!" She had not had a drink in a while, she was parched. I got her another cupful, that brought her around a little more. "Where are you headed?"

She said, "Charleston."

"Are you walking all that way?" I said startled.

"Is it that far away?" I was not sure if she just had no idea where Charleston was or if she just did not want to say because she had no real destination. She clearly was not from around here. I asked her if she had any money. She could ride the bus. "No, I do not." She said, as she looked down feeling embarrassed.

I got up and walked over to the bus driver. "Sir, I was wondering if we could help this lady. She is walking, and she says she is headed to Charleston." He looked around me over at her.

He said, "Can she pay for a ticket?"

I said, "I will cover the ticket when we get to my destination. We can't just let her walk all that way. There are plenty of empty seats. I promise I will take care of it."

He looked around me, at her again, with a crooked mouth and an annoyed look. "Okay, I guess. But I expect payment when we get there."

"Yes, sir, thank you," I said excitedly. Now I just need to get the money from Aunt Mags. I definitely could not pay for that ticket. But I know Aunt Mags, she would help her, I hope.

I walked back over to the lady. She was leaned back and looked like she had passed out. I grabbed her a Nehi in the station before going to tell her I secured a seat on the bus for her. When I came back out, she had disappeared. The driver was telling everyone it was time to go. I looked around and spotted her across the parking lot, headed back out to walk. "Hey, hey! Lady, wait!" I shouted. She did not stop, so I ran after her. "Hey, lady!" I shouted as I caught her. "I got you a seat on the bus. You don't need to walk!"

"What? Are you daft? I haven't any money."

"I told the driver we will take care of it when we get to my destination. My Aunt Mags will help. She is always helping people in need."

"I can't take your money."

"Well, technically we aren't giving it to you. We are giving it to Greyhound." I chuckled. She looked at me and rolled her eyes.

"True. Okay, if you think it is okay."

I said, "Sure, I know she will help. Let's go, everyone is getting on." We ran back to the bus. We got on. The bus driver gave us an annoyed look and closed the doors behind us. I showed her back to the seat where I was sitting. "Oh, here I got you a Nehi!"

"Nehi?" she said. "What is that?"

"Just the best drink ever! Here try it," I said.

"Hmm, interesting, it is very sweet and purple. It is decent."

"Are you hungry? My Momma packed me a pimento sandwich if you would like it."

"Pimento?" she questioned.

"Yeah. Just like a cheese spread for bread." I started looking in my bag for the wax wrapped sandwich. "By the way, what is your name?"

As I handed her the sandwich, she took a bite, looked up, and while in midchew said, "Elizabeth."

"Nice to meet you, I am Katie." She ate that sandwich like she had not eaten in quite some time. When she finished, she said, "That was quite good. I feel a bit more like myself now. Thank you for your aid."

"No problem, it is my way of paying all the people back that ever helped me, my pleasure." She fell asleep almost immediately after our conversation. I looked over to ask her where she was from, and she had fallen fast asleep.

Chapter 18

Is she breathing? I thought to myself. I looked steadily at her face. She had not moved, and I was trying to look closely to see if I could tell if she was. As I slowly stuck my finger out to put under her nose to check for air, she awoke and swatted at my hand. "What are you doing?" she said startled.

"Sorry, I was just checking to see if you were still with us. You were sleeping so deeply."

"Yes, I am much better now. I have not slept in a few days."

"Are you from around here, Elizabeth? I mean, I know, not originally, obviously…but—"

"I understand what you mean," Elizabeth interrupts. "I have been living in Georgia with a sponsor family for the last few months. Nice elderly couple," she stopped. I was looking at her intently for the whole story, waiting for more information. But she was playing it close to the cuff. Of course, I am a stranger to her. She completely clammed up. I don't blame her. I would do the same thing. I decided to try to finish off my Nehi and enjoy the ride.

We got closer to my stop. I decided to try to ask a little more information. I wondered why she was here. Did she know anyone? Did she have somewhere to stay? Why did she leave Georgia?

"Elizabeth," I started. "Do you have someone you are meeting?"

"Well, not exactly," she said. "You know you could stay with my aunt and I. She has a B&B."

"But I have no money. I don't take charity," she said sternly.

"Maybe…you could do some odd jobs for your stay."

She looked away in thought. "I could help with the cleaning and cooking. It would not be for long. I need to rest, and then I will move on."

"I am sure my aunt won't mind, and she will need the help now that the holidays are over."

She thought for a moment. "Okay, I appreciate your kindness." She looked away as her eyes started to water.

I put my hand on hers. "It's okay. I am happy to help if I can." I'm sure there was more to her story, would have to wait to find out later.

As we pulled into the bus terminal, I spotted Aunt Mags and Miss Millie, so happy to finally be here. Now, I had some fast talking to do to acquire the money for her ticket and a job and place to stay for Elizabeth. I hope Aunt Mags was as generous as I had seen in the past. We filed off the bus, and I told Elizabeth to follow me. The driver stopped us and said I need the money. I said, "Okay hold on, I need to speak to my aunt."

He said, "Okay, but she stays with me until its paid." Elizabeth looked at me in fear. I am sure she was scared to death.

"Hold on, I promise I will be right back." I ran up to Aunt Mags and explained, in short, all the events of the past few hours.

She looked toward the bus and looked at me like "what am I getting myself into?" "Okay, we can't leave the girl in Greyhound jail. That would be horrible. Go get her."

I hugged her quickly, she handed me the money for her ticket, and I ran back to the bus. "Here you go, sir, paid in full!" I said, happily smiling at Elizabeth. She looked relieved. He nodded, and we exited the bus.

The smell of diesel was strong as the bus pulled away. I walked up to Aunt Mags and introduced Elizabeth to her and Miss Millie. "This is Elizabeth," I started to say.

She interrupted, "Elizabeth Foyle, mum," reaching out her hand for a shake.

"Hello, Elizabeth, nice to meet you," Aunt Mags said. "I hear you will be staying with us for a little while."

"Yes, if you don't mind. I don't have any money, but I can offer my services in retribution."

"That should work out fine. I was looking to hire someone for cleaning and helping Miss Millie with the meals. You can stay on as long as you need."

"Thank you, mum," she said as she lowered her head.

"Now, let's go back to the house. We have dinner cooking, and then we can rest and plan for our boarders coming in the next couple of days. We need to get Elizabeth settled in too," Aunt Mags said as she welcomed in the perfect stranger with a smile and a hug like she had known her forever. She never ceased to amaze me. We sang to the radio all the way to the house.

I was so consumed with this new situation I seemed to forget my current one and the interviews I needed to prepare for. It kind of puts things in perspective when you help others and realize there are more important things to take care of than your own little world.

We reached the house, and once we got inside, I gave Elizabeth the tour. Aunt Mags said to let her pick her room. Of course, she picked the English-themed room. She said it was comforting and reminded her of her own room. This time, I picked the French-themed room. It was pretty and elegant. Also their food is mild, so if they take my room as a hint of what food I want, it won't be so spicy this time.

We all met downstairs. We talked into the night, and Elizabeth told us her story and other stories she had heard while in England. She went through so much, I told her she should write a book. She was a great storyteller, like Aunt Mags. Over the next few days and weeks, we would learn much more about Elizabeth and become new best friends.

Chapter 19

Those first few days flew by after I arrived at Aunt Mags's house. I helped with the cleaning, cooking, for the new boarders. It was time for me to get up and get ready to go to my interview. I was nervous and went over my list of questions, one last time, from Mrs. Vance. That helped a lot. Aunt Mags let me take the car. I enjoyed the ride into town. It was sunny but a little chilly, so my suit was perfect. I had my pearls on and my charm bracelet. So I had everyone with me to support me in spirit. I parked down the street. I put on my last layer of lipstick, checked my hair, and began my walk to the store.

The shop front was so pretty, large windows with the mannequins in the latest styles. Utilitarian and practical, extravagance was not in style. I loved the accessories and details in the windows. I walked in, and the bell on the door rang. Two girls were working to change some displays in the front, and the manager came out to greet me. "Welcome, you must be Katie?"

"Yes, ma'am," I responded.

"And you are early. I do love punctuality. Some people could learn from your example," she said a little loudly. The other shop girls looked at her and rolled their eyes. She gave them the side eye. "Step back here in my office, and we will chat a few minutes. I won't keep you long." I nervously walked behind her, not knowing what to expect. "My name is Geraldine Songer. I have managed the store now for five years. I live in Mt. Pleasant, and I'm here every day except Sunday and Monday. We are closed on Sundays. I have a few girls that work here and rotate hours. I am trying to provide work for as many as I can, but you won't get many hours, starting out. Right now, sales are slow, and rationing is causing issues getting merchandise. But we will stay open as long as we can. It won't last forever, we hope. Right?"

"Yes, ma'am," I said. She asked if I had anyone serving in the military.

I said, "Yes, my brother and a close friend and several other friends from home."

She asked, "Where is home?"

I responded, "Right now, Isle of Palm with my aunt. Originally I am from a town, just south of Edisto. My momma and pops are still there."

She looked at me with a smile. "That is a blessing, to still have your parents. I miss mine every day. Okay, so let's get to the hard questions," she said in a business voice. We talked for about thirty minutes, and then she said, "I have a few more girls to interview today. But I plan on making a decision this evening. I will give a call to the one I choose this evening so they can come in tomorrow for training. That will give them time to be ready to go on Monday. I enjoyed meeting you. Good luck!" She reached out to shake my hand. Some of her questions made me really think.

My next interview was not for a couple of hours, and it was a few blocks away. I was so hungry. I heard my stomach growl during the interview. I found a diner that looked busy, so it had to be good. I needed a plate of fries. Finding a place to park the car, I went inside. The waitress seated me, and my fries and malt were delivered in record time. "Could I get a bottle of ketchup?"

I closed my eyes for just a minute, trying to find some quiet in my noisy head, and suddenly heard someone say, "Katie?"

Slowly opening my eyes, there was Grumps. "Hey! Yeah! It is me," I said.

"What are you doing here?" he questioned.

"I am in town for interviews for work."

"Seeing your aunt's car outside, I thought she was here."

"Nope, just me, sorry to disappoint," I said kind of annoyed, continuing to enjoy my meal.

"Oh, I did not mean it like that. I only came in to say hi," he said awkwardly.

"You came to say hi to my aunt, but it is her immature niece Katie is what you mean. So you feel obligated to say hello. Well, hello and goodbye, I need to go to my next interview. I will give my aunt your hello." I left my money on the table and made my exit.

As I walked away, he just kind of stood there, not sure what to say except, "I did not mean it that way." I was not going to give him the satisfaction of forgiveness. After I left, I got in my car and pulled out. I saw him in the rear view, standing outside the diner looking a little lost. Maybe I was a little hard on him. But he has not been the kindest person to me. Not to mention, he interrupted my meal and brief moment of meditation. There also was no explanation of the bloody shirt yet. Now that we are in the same city, we probably would see more of each other. I will be a little nicer, next time, maybe.

Anyway, I was off to my next interview. It was in a much bigger store, more like a department store. After a long tour and a barrage of questions and inappropriate comments, the manager was gruff and condescending. I liked the smaller store better. I would just hope Mrs. Songer would call me back. The manager at the second place was kind of creepy. If she did not call, I would be back to the drawing board and put in more applications.

After the last interview, I headed over to Station 18 to sit on my favorite beach for just a few minutes before heading back. The traffic was heavy that time of the day. It took a while to get to the beach area. Once I arrived, I parked along the street, a block over from the entry. I then removed my shoes and stockings and my suit jacket before walking on to the sand so I would not get too hot. I was sitting there on the old log, enjoying the sand and breeze when a dog, a yellow lab, came running up to me unsupervised, it seemed. I looked, no one was around. "Where is your owner, boy? You should not be out here alone."

Someone in the distance was hollering from over the dunes, "Sport, Sport! Where are you?" the mysterious voice said. I looked back, and a man was coming over the dunes with an empty leash. I grabbed the dog by the collar so he would not run off. As he got closer, I realized it was Grumps. What is happening? Is he following me? "Katie, what are you doing here? How do we keep running into each other?" he said.

"Is this your dog? "No, I am house sitting for a friend. He warned me he would escape off the leash. Sorry, he attacked you."

"No, he is fine," I said.

"You are out here in your work clothes?"

"Sort of."

As he looked down, seeing my stockings and shoes sitting beside me, he smiled. "Well, you can't come to the beach and not put your feet in the sand."

I said, slightly embarrassed, "You know, after all this time, I still don't know your name."

He smiled and said, "It is Ben."

"I am sorry, Ben, I was so rude to you earlier in the day. I had no reason to act like that, no matter how you have acted toward me in the past."

"Yeah, about that," he said, "I am sorry if I was rude when I was at the B&B. I was going through some stuff, shouldn't have been so unpleasant."

"Okay, we are all caught up on apologies now," I said kind of relieved. "Maybe, we can be friends, since it seems we will be running into each other more. Truce?"

"Yes, truce. Well, come on, Sport, time to go," he said.

"I need to get going too. I need to get back to my aunt's."

"Oh, are you living at the B&B now?" he said.

"Yeah. It is much closer, if I get one of the jobs I interviewed for," I replied.

"Well good luck, and safe travels. Tell your aunt I said hello, again." He smiled, recalling what I had said at the diner. I looked up at him and returned the smile. He put the leash back on the dog. I reached over to pick up my shoes and stockings. I looked up, and he had reached out his hand to help me up. "Thank you," I said. Then he turned to walk away. Usually, I am the one walking away first. He is easy on the eyes. I felt good about our truce. I still had lots of questions. But it just didn't seem like the right time. I think we could be good friends, in time. I headed back to Isle of Palm with a day's worth of events to tell everyone and to record in my journal.

Chapter 20

I arrived back at the house, and my aunt met me at the door. She appeared very upset. "What is wrong?" I said. "What happened?"

She said, "Come in, and sit down."

"What? You are scaring me." I said a little louder.

"Your dad called and said that they got notice your brother had been injured. They are not sure how bad it is yet. But they are stabilizing him and sending him here to the Naval Hospital in Charleston."

"Oh no. Should I go home? Is Momma okay?"

"Your dad said don't come home. Everything is okay. She is upset, but it could be worse. Most of his troop died in the attack. So he was a lucky one. They want you here so you can check in on him at the hospital." I felt dazed, thinking the worst, and it still could be bad, searching my thoughts about how to process all this, still not hearing from Luke either. My letters trailed off from Rebecca, probably because of school and interning at a local hospital. God only knows the horrors she saw, not to mention the horrors seen by the soldiers coming home.

I had been talking to Elizabeth. She told me some things she witnessed herself. She would wake up with nightmares sometimes. If I heard her, I would get up with her until she would get tired and go back to sleep. War is a horrible thing to have to experience. Liz told us one evening at dinner about a bunch of American soldiers that came into their business. She said they were kind and polite. One of them had been talking to her and came back in the store a couple of times. "The last time I saw him was the evening our business got bombed and destroyed. We'd just left to go home, a few hours before it happened. They were getting ready to be shipped out too. So he told me to write him, he lives here in Charleston. But I forgot his address at the shop, so all I had been the city and state, lost in the fire that consumed the store.

"My parents decided to send me here to the states. Our church found placement with a church here and a family just till they could get settled somewhere or find some way to get here too. I feel bad for leaving the kind couple I've been staying with, and I know they're concerned about me. But they said I could go, and if I ever needed, I would be welcomed to come back. Being elderly, they knew I needed to make my way. I am not sure what happened to my parents. We lost contact with them. So I decided not to wait but go ahead with my life." Liz was so brave, reminded me of Rebecca. She knew what she wanted or at least the direction she was going. Helping at the B&B, she became invaluable. Fate had made us fast friends.

"Liz! I have an idea!" I said while we fixed dinner. My mind, still racing, thinking about my brother and what condition he was.

"What idea is that, Katie?" she said.

"I think we should volunteer at the hospital on our days off. We might find someone who knows your GI? I can check on my brother too once he gets here."

"That sounds wonderful!" She smiled. "I would love to help!"

"Yeah, me too. Maybe I can find someone that knows where Luke is too." I told her all about him. She said our story sounded like a movie. I'm beginning to wonder how this movie would end.

"Katie, phone is for you!" Aunt Mags said. I put down the plates and silverware I was arranging and went to the phone. Aunt Mags shrugged her shoulders as I approached her with a quizzical look on my face. She did not know who was on the phone, I picked it up, Mrs. Songer.

"Yes, ma'am, thank you so much. I will see you tomorrow." Aunt Mags, Liz, and Miss Millie all waited anxiously. "I got the job!" We all celebrated, and Aunt Mags got out the strawberry wine that evening, bittersweet to celebrate with everything going on, but it lifted out spirits. Miss Millie went to bed, and we sat in the living room, reading and talking.

Aunt Mags said, "I have something I want to talk to you about." She looked so serious. "I am going to need my car. So you are going to need to get one of your own." I felt panic set in. I start work tomorrow. What am I gonna do? She said, "I want to make you a deal."

"Okay? What is the deal? I have my old car out in the other garage. There is nothing wrong with it, just needs cleaning up and maybe a tune up. I am not giving it to you. You will need to pay me until it is paid off."

"Oh yes! Yes! Thank you!" I jumped up and hugged her neck. Liz was so happy for me. I told her I would share it with her.

She smiled. "I have not driven in some time, may need some practice."

"We can definitely practice," I said.

I could hardly contain my excitement—new job, a car, volunteering at the hospital. Aunt Mags was going to check on the volunteering at the hospital and would let me know. Tomorrow is the first day on my way to a new adventure. Maybe Liz would find her GI. Maybe I would find mine too! Only time will tell.

Thinking about my brother brought thoughts about missing Luke, especially after not hearing from him in several months. Spring arriving soon, and I remembered spending time with Luke at the fair. I decided to go up to the roof to see if I could find our star. The night was especially dark, and I had the telescope so I could see things clearer. Where could he be? Why had I not heard from him? Maybe he was over me finally. Should I move on? I am sure someone else will come along. What if that was my one chance? Like Aunt Mags, she had one great love, there has to be more. Luke, where are you?

As I searched the night sky, my mind started wandering, thinking about the day and all that happened. The bizarre meeting with Ben, now that I know his name. I'm glad we agreed to a truce, assured there is so much more to him. He seemed like a completely different person today than he was here at the B&B. I guess you should not be quick to judge someone. You never know what they are going through. I am learning to get out of my little world. I want to get involved at the hospital. My aunt said at dinner that they are trying to get together a USO-type entertainment for the patients there to help with morale of the soldiers and the staff that are there dealing with a lot. They think it would be a welcome distraction to their pain and daily thoughts. I would love to help with the entertainment. I am only working part-time. So I would love to help in the weekends. I need to get some songs together and start practicing. Elizabeth and I can start working on a list of songs. She can teach me some new ones she knows I could use. Maybe this journey will help us find her GI in all this madness.

Chapter 21

By this time, I had been working at the shop for a month. It was spring, and we styled the newest fashions to put in the windows. Everything was very boxy shaped and suits and practical outfits the fashion. The suits, smart and military looking, but it made us all feel like we were a part. It was hard to understand and deal with the thought that life just went on even though there were people in the middle of a war or conflict in so many places in the world. Life just kept going here at home. Nothing felt normal, so many of our family members and loved ones overseas going through only things we would read about or see a little in the movie theater.

On a daily basis, there was news of their family members being injured, or worse MIA or POW, to me, might be the worst. The not knowing, the constant torture of wondering, we heard of victories overseas but at great expense of so many lives.

My brother finally made it back. He is at the Naval Hospital. I got to go see him just a couple of days after he got back. He was heavily sedated with major damage to both legs. I walked in that first day, happy to be able to see him but not sure what to expect. The nurse spoke with us before we went in. He was in a large ward area with other GIs, also injured. We were told to be quiet. She tried to prepare us for what we might see. When my aunt and I walked in, beds lined both sides of the long room. It was quiet. All you could hear was the bustling of the nurses and people in white walking from bed to bed, doing various tasks. They hardly ever looked up, very intent and busy caring for all the wounded. I saw a doctor standing by the bed the nurse directed us to. He examined the solider as we approached. As we got closer, the nurse said, "Doctor, this is Michael's family." He stood up and turned around. It was Ben!

I stopped in my tracks. My aunt said, "Hey, we know you." He looked as surprised as we were.

I said, "That is my brother." I walked up and grabbed Mickie's hand.

Ben said, "He is heavily sedated. He had a few surgeries and will be going in again in the morning. I am one of the surgeons here at the hospital."

My mind went back to that night I saw him at the B&B. Now his appearance that night totally made sense, his overall demeanor during his stay totally understandable. We had no idea what he was going through. I suddenly felt bad for thinking and treating him like I did. Reliving all those conversations with him, I felt like a heel.

He began to explain my brother's condition. It was serious, but he would recuperate, barring any infections. He had a long rehabilitation ahead to learn to walk again. He would be here at the hospital for some time. They have rehabilitation facility too for those that require a longer stay. I was relieved to finally see him. So glad he was back, but I was also worried about his condition physically and mentally.

We returned home that evening after a long day at the hospital. I sat in on some meetings my aunt conducted regarding the USO shows. Things were working out, and we could begin gathering acts and musicians soon. There was a letter when we got back waiting for me in the mail. I finally heard from Rebecca. She graduated and now working at Walter Reed which happened to be one of the most active army hospitals in the country. She was always looking for guys we grew up with to come through, finding a few but no word on Luke. She told me there was not only physical injury but such trauma of the mind and soul, a lot of head trauma, injuries, and amputations. Befriending a couple that were unidentifiable due to burns or injuries to their memory made her so sad. The hospital offered counseling and classes to help deal with all this as well. She said it was like a whole other world there in the hospital. She sent me a pic of her outside the hospital in her nurse uniform with a couple of the patients she took care of. She looked wonderful but so tired and grown-up now. I can't imagine what she was going through. I was glad to hear from her. She mentioned falling for one of the soldiers that had head trauma. It was mostly his memory. But she cared for him daily and said he was such a kind person. She sounded serious about this guy. She never really talked about anyone that way before. He must be pretty special.

I wrote her back about Ben and how I am sure he had a bigger story, but I had not had a chance to figure him out yet. I also explained to Liz what happened at the hospital and our encounters before that. "I was so surprised it was Ben."

Liz said, "I bet that was a shock. How is your brother?"

"He looks beat up. We could not see his legs. They were all bandaged. I am worried that he might get worse. They said there was a chance of infection."

Liz assured me, "He will be fine. It sounds like he has an excellent doctor." She smiled. I glanced at her with a side smile.

"You know, I sat and watched Ben as I sat with my brother. Mickie was totally out of it, but I sat with him for a while and held his hand. So he knew I was there. I watched Ben with the other patients. He was so gentle and kind with each one. I noticed he had a bit of a limp when he walked. He was cutting up with a few of them. I am curious to know more about him and his story."

Liz said, "Yes, it does sound interesting." She smiled and raised her eyebrows. "Does he have a brother?" Liz asked. She could tell I was not paying attention.

"What?" I started daydreaming again, thinking back to the day on the beach, remembering him sitting in that chair just across the room on that late night, no doubt exhausted from a horrible day at the hospital. He went through all that alone, without any of us knowing. I know his mother passed. I wondered if he had other family. I need to find time to talk to him. "I am not sure if he has a brother, but I will definitely find out for you." I smiled. I am intrigued now. It was time for bed. I had a big week coming up with work and going with Aunt Mags to meetings about the USO show, seems like the tides changed and might reveal some special things ahead.

I headed to work the next morning. I only worked half a day and then was to meet Aunt Mags and Liz at the hospital. I wanted to check on Mickie since he had that surgery and hoped he would be conscious. The morning seemed to fly by. I tried to stay busy. I then headed over to the hospital, walked in, and got to the ward. There was Mickie. He appeared to be awake. I walked up to him. He said, "Hey, Katie. It is so good to see you. Aunt Mags was in here a few min ago with your friend Liz. She was very interesting."

"Mickie, are you okay? I was so worried about you."

Mickie smiled. "Yeah, they say I will be fine, but it will take a while. They say it was a land mine. Several of my buddies did not make it. All I remember is walking through a field, the whole troop, and then nothing. I woke up and my legs mangled, and I was in shock and excruciating pain. They evacuated me out as quick as they could. I lost consciousness at some point and lost a lot of blood. They thought they would have to amputate, but I begged them not to. Then I just remember winding up here. This doctor working on me is supposed to be the best. He was a field surgeon at some point and got injured. They sent him back here, and he has been working here ever since. The nurses say he is the best. They say I am in good hands."

I smiled. "Mickie, are you okay?"

He looked at me the smile faded. He said, "I have nightmares, wake up in sweats. Some other guys here wake up screaming. It is horrible. I saw things you can't imagine. But I am working through it. Now, about that friend of yours. She is beautiful."

"Down, boy. You need to concentrate on getting better." I rolled my eyes. "I need to go find Aunt Mags. We have a meeting with the hospital director about the USO show we wanted to do for the soldiers on the weekends to help with morale. Maybe you can talk to Liz at those. But you need to get better."

"Okay, Katie," he smiled like he was up to something. Of course, he was.

Chapter 22

Where are they? I looked in a couple of offices trying to find Aunt Mags and Liz. I found the auditorium and decided to go in and check out the room. As I walked in, I heard music. Someone was playing piano, and very well I might add. I stood there quietly to hear what it was. They were playing "You'll Never Know." You could feel the emotion in their playing. I walked further into the room to see who it was. They might be a good choice for accompaniment in the show. To my surprise, it was Ben. I stood just out of sight. He had his eyes closed while he was playing really getting into the song. It was beautiful. He was a great surgeon and a piano player. What a gift to have those talents.

When he finished, he slowly closed the lid on the keys, put both hands on the bench, and dropped his head. I walked up to the stage out of the shadows. "That was something to watch," I said.

He looked up, shocked that I was there. "Now, who is stalking who? Did you see your brother?" he said.

"Yes, I stopped there first. I was looking for Aunt Mags," I said in my defense.

He said, "Yes, they were just here with the director, right as I was coming in. I come in here during my free time when I get a chance. Playing helps me escape." He rubbed his eyes. "I used to play classical, but the newer songs are short, less intense, and have a lighter feel to them."

I walked up on the stage, then over to the piano. I leaned over on the piano. "I could tell. I could feel it too. You know we are looking for acts to fill in for the show. Would you be interested? I am sure the patients would be impressed that their doctor had other talents other than repairing their injuries. Your playing might help in other ways too."

"Oh, I don't know. I don't play to entertain. It is just to relax," he said.

"I understand. I said the same thing about singing. I sang at home and sometimes at the nursing home and the VFW on special occasions. It really seemed to transport the people listening, and they enjoyed it. I felt like I was helping them the only way I knew how," I explained. "You have the gift of repairing their bodies and now possibly their hearts and minds with your talent of playing music. It would be a shame to waste that," I said.

He looked at me. "Are you done with your speech now?"

"Sorry, did not mean to sound bossy. Just want you to consider."

He smiled. "Okay, I will think about it. You have made a compelling argument."

I smiled with a proud undertone. "Well, get a list of possible songs you might want to perform, and I will let Aunt Mags know." I stood to leave.

Ben stood up and said, "Wait, would you be interested in getting dinner with me one evening? You know, to discuss the show, I would like to help."

A smile came across my face. I couldn't fight it. "Yes, that sounds nice." Right then, I thought of Luke. I had those similar feelings I had with Luke. I dialed it back a little. "Maybe you can just come to my aunt's one evening. We can have dinner there." He acted a little disappointed. He said, "Oh sure, we can do that."

"Okay, so I will check with my aunt and let you know. I have to go find her now for some meetings. Have a good day."

"You too, Katie," he replied. I left quickly. I needed to get out of there. I had to shake that feeling. I don't even know him yet, so why do I feel guilty? We agreed to move on. Luke must have moved on since I have not heard from him in months.

Aunt Mags and Liz were coming down the hallway. She said, "That was good timing. We are headed to the conference room now. Are you okay?" Liz said, "You look like you saw a ghost."

"I didn't see one, but I felt one," I said to myself.

"What?" Liz said.

"Never mind, I am fine."

Aunt Mags flashed a quick smile. Then she said, "We won't be long. Then we can head into Charleston for a movie or a show. It'll be fun. I think Casablanca is still playing. I hear it is really good!!" It had been so long since Liz had seen a movie. She was excited. I was still distracted.

Our meeting went well, and my aunt was confirming the acts for next weekend. I volunteered to be in the first wave, just a couple of songs. We wanted to leave some time for the band to just play music so those who could dance would get the chance. We were looking for a dance group or comedian that could perform too. My aunt had some leads she was following up on. We will try to keep it down to two hours the first shows and see how that goes.

We then headed into Charleston to the movie theatre. We stopped at the general store and grabbed a few Nehi drinks. Liz was hooked from her first one. We then grabbed some popcorn on the way in to the theater. I loved the previews and the news reels they had before the movies. I always searched the screen for Luke's face, just a glimpse to know he was okay. Liz even mentioned later she was looking for her GI in the reels too.

The movie was so good. It was exciting and action packed, a nice distraction from the real world. I heard one of my favorite songs in the film too, "As Time Goes By." I like the Jimmy Durante version of the song. Humphrey and Ingrid really had chemistry. She looked so pretty in the film too, makes you wonder if they secretly liked each other during the film.

We headed home after it was over. We had a full day. And the coming week would be filled with work, practice for the show, visiting with Mickie, and planning a dinner for Ben. I wonder what his favorite food was. What would I wear? This was just a working dinner. What was I thinking? I was so torn between the past and the possibilities of the future.

I ran upstairs to Liz's room. I knocked. "Hey are you still awake?"

"Yeah, come on in," Liz said.

"So I am supposed to have dinner with Ben."

"Oh really."

"Yes, I think he wanted to take me out, but I told him we could eat here."

"What? Why would you say that? Let him wine and dine you."

"I don't know if I am ready to be wined and dined."

"Okay, think about it. You have not heard from Luke. You said had the talk before he left, so you both were free to move on."

"Yeah, but saying it and doing it are two different things," I said. "My heart and mind kept drifting back to Luke, but I know I need to move on."

Liz said, "You are always talking about moving forward. Don't look back. Life is so short, Katie. I learned that while I was still in England. Friends and family would be alive, and well, one moment, and the next thing you know they were gone, sometimes within hours of last seeing them. It was almost impossible to believe, hardly even time to grieve. That taught me to live one day at a time. Absorb all you can from that day and remember, always remember, but keep moving forward."

"Yeah, Pops said to always remember, 'Life is like the tide. It will pull you under, and you will sink if you stand still.' I saw my Momma do that when my brother left. She started moving forward again when I went back home and got better. I understand."

"It will all work out," Liz said. "We will find our way and the one we are supposed to love." I started to tear up, and she gave me a hug. "We will get through this."

"Thank you, Liz. I am so glad our paths crossed. You were sent along just in time."

"I feel the same way, Katie."

"It is getting late. We need our beauty rest."

"Goodnight, Liz."

"Goodnight, Katie."

Chapter 23

The countdown began, and I should be nervous, so many details, and responsibilities that I need to take care of before the weekend show, helps to reduce my nerves somehow. First, a full day at the shop, I am learning a lot about business and merchandising from Mrs. Songer. She turned into a mentor in this learning experience of employment, kind of my very own resident, Mrs. Vance, from back home. She said I am a quick learner, and the customers like the added attention I give them, gives me a sense of accomplishment and satisfaction knowing some of them ask for me when they visit in the store. I like my job here, and most of the girls are great to work with. A couple of questionable characters I had run-ins with, but I think I held my own.

Times are competitive in this line of work, especially since we make extra commission on sales. We are given limited hours, so opportunities are scarce, in the current economy, even more of a challenge. We are lucky we live in this big city. I have a better chance here than if I were at home. Momma said several of the shops in town had to close due to low demand for unnecessary products or things that are being rationed.

That reminds me, I need to pick them up at the bus depot on Friday evening. They are coming to visit for a couple of days. They wanted to come sooner, but I told Pops to wait for Mickie to heal a little more before Momma saw him. I did not want to upset her too much. He had so many surgeries to repair his legs. But he has the best doctor. An unconscious smile appears on my face. I think I could like Ben. I know, I know I don't really know him yet, yet moving forward, not standing still. I am kind of fond of my new shoes, to let them get sucked into the surf. I looked down at my new shoes, smiled, and got back to work.

After work, I decided to stop at the diner down the street before I headed to the hospital to Mickie and to rehearse with the band and performers for the show. I decided to eat my favorite plate of fries and a chocolate malt. Rebecca had been on my mind lately, not heard from her in a while. With kind of work, she is always busy. I wondered about her, and the GI she was falling for. Wanting to share with her my feelings about Ben, I needed her hardcore thoughts. I called a week or so ago and left a message with her Mom to have her call me. I am sure she will call soon.

I finished up my less-than-healthy meal and felt energized to tackle these rehearsals. Arriving at the hospital, I notice cars and musicians coming in and out of the loading entrance with instruments and stands. My aunt had hired a catering group to provide food for the evening. That way, there would be no undue stress on the hospital staff. She was so good at organizing and thinking about all the little details that were very important. Luckily, the auditorium was on the opposite end of the ward area. We could get things in place. The noise would be minimal, and the surprise would be better.

I headed to see Mickie. I walked in his ward, and his bed was empty. I got a little concerned. I located one of his nurses and asked where he was. She said, "Hi, Katie, they just took him to the rehab room, down the hall, turn right, then two doors down, on the right."

"Oh okay, thank you." I put my hand on my heart.

She laughed. "Oh, don't worry he is too ornery for anything bad to happen to him."

I said, "I know that is right."

I headed down the hallway and found the room. I walked in, and there he was, on the hand rails trying to stand. To my surprise, Liz was there too. "Hey, you two," I exclaimed. She was standing just beside him, cheering him on.

"Hey, Katie," my brother grunted as he was struggling to stand. "I was just going for a jog."

"I noticed that. Liz you might not be able to keep up with him once he gets going. He ran track in school."

She looked at me concerned and quickly joined in on the dream of him walking, even running again someday. "I am sure I will not be able to keep up," she said. He was grunting and straining to just lift himself from the chair. He had recently begun rehab and gaining arm strength. Long road ahead, but he is determined, looks like he may have some unexpected inspiration too. I was not aware of him and Liz being a thing yet.

I am glad they have found each other, if not forever, at least for now. Mickie needs someone to tame his wild side, and she needs someone who is a free spirit like Mickie. He will need her to help him through these days of regaining his strength, and I think she can give him something to work for. She still has some trauma of her own. That is something they have in common.

I stayed for a few minutes, then headed down to the auditorium. You could faintly hear the band practicing. They sounded great. My Aunt had told me they found a tap-dancing couple that were going to do a performance to "Boogie Woogie Bugle Boy" of Company B and "Yankee Doodle Dandy" and the grand finale, a dance routine of "Jukebox Dance" by Cole Porter. I had seen them audition, they were fantastic. They will bring down the house, bursting, full of energy.

I finally reached the auditorium and found the guys taking a break, and Ben was on stage playing the piano in his scrubs. He was on break from surgery. He was softly playing while the room bustled with activity. He was in his zone again, eyes closed, head down, losing himself even for just a few minutes, far from the constant madness of fixing all these broken men and women. He was playing "All for You," nice slow dance song. Some of the band picked up their instruments and started playing along. It was like he did not hear them though. He never looked up. I sat in the chairs listening and waiting for him to finish.

Aunt Mags came in the door behind me and said, "There you are. I have some mail you might want."

I looked at her wide-eyed. "Thank you!" I looked through it but nothing from Luke, only Rebecca. I was glad but disappointed at the same time. I would have to wait to read the letter because the band was ready for me to practice. Ben was coming down off the stage as I was going up. He looked so tired. "Hey, how are you?" I asked.

"Doing well, just a long few days, lots of casualties coming in that had some complications. Most are doing okay. I lost a few too though. That never gets easier. They all look so young," he said wearily.

"I had an idea for dinner on Thursday evening."

"We are still on for dinner at your aunt's?"

"Oh! yeah, we are definitely still on for dinner," I said anxiously.

"Well, I was thinking, would you meet me at the open-air market in town so we can buy some fresh vegetables? I want to cook for you. My mother's spaghetti recipe, an old recipe and her side of the family, was genuine Italian. So it is very authentic." He perked up a bit while telling me.

"That sounds wonderful. I can make dessert. I have the perfect Italian dessert to go with your meal. I will keep it a surprise."

"Sounds like a plan then." He smiled. "See you Thursday evening, at your shop. We can go from there," he said as he continued down the stairs.

"I am looking forward to it," I said a little loudly.

Everyone turned to see what the shouting was about, including Ben. He stopped and turned back and said with a smile, "I am too."

I did my couple of numbers with the band. The band was spectacular. They had the cardboard stands with the name of the band on front, reminded me of Glenn Miller or Benny Goodman's bands. They had all been playing together for some time now. Just a couple more acts, and Aunt Mags needed a ride home. I told her I would wait for her. After the dancing couple, I walked out into the courtyard of the hospital where some soldiers sat or walked around assisted by nurses. A nice tranquil place to step away outside and enjoy the evening or what was left of it. I sat outside for about an hour, watching the men and nurses. The sky was clear. Only small lanterns lit the courtyard, so you could look up and gaze at the stars. I leaned back and looked for that bright star, wondering what had become of Luke. I did not dare think the worst. I am sure he was just out of reach or had decided to move on. Coming to that realization, I was feeling the urge to move on myself. As I sat stargazing, I hear, "Can we share a seat?" It was Ben. I secretly hoped I would see him again, but I knew he was working. "What are you still doing here?" he asked.

"I am waiting on Aunt Mags. Elizabeth had to hurry back to the B&B to help Miss Millie with dinner for the boarders. Aunt Mags had to finish some set up and finish watching the acts. I decided to come out for some fresh air. Beautiful night. Look at those stars, so clear tonight."

"Oh look, a shooting star," as he pointed.

"Make a wish," I said. Ben then said something I had never thought of but was true.

"Ever wonder why we wish on something that is nearing its end?"

"What do you mean?" I said puzzled.

"A shooting star is actually a piece of a meteor that is burning up and disintegrating on entry to the earth. Most of the time, they never reach the earth surface. They just burn up. I want to wish on a star that is fixed in the sky that I know will be there when I look for it," he explained. "Something I can really hang my dreams on." He smiled.

"You are right, I never thought of it that way," I said as I leaned back further to observe the night sky, my feet crossed and in the air.

He placed his hand on my back to catch me as I leaned further. "Be careful you might fall." I sat up quickly and looked over at him. He was sitting closer to me now. He said, "Would you mind if I kissed you?" I could not say a word, but I shook my head no ever so slightly. He moved in slowly and kissed me. If there is such a thing as a sincere kiss, that is what that was. You could tell he had put a lot of thought into it beforehand. I don't recall ever being kissed like that before. It was enchanting. I know that sounds corny, but it was. I can't say that I had not thought about kissing him before, but nothing like this. He whispered, "I had wanted to do that for quite a while."

I whispered back, "I am so glad you did."

Aunt Mags suddenly appeared and said, "Hey, Katie, you out here?"

I stood up and composed myself. "I am here, Aunt Mags."

"Oh, there you are. Ben, how are you this beautiful evening?"

"Very well, Maggie." He smiled and looked down. "Just completed my shift, and Katie was sitting here as I was leaving, thought I would sit for a spell with her."

"Well, thank you for keeping an eye on her," Aunt Mags said cheerfully. "Y'all say your goodbyes. I have had a long day. My dogs are barkin'." She headed off to the car, waving her hand as she walked away.

Ben looked at me and said, "Good night." He smiled and leaned in. This time, he took me in his arms and kissed me, talking about seeing stars. I think I was falling but no burning up on reentry to earth for this girl. "Good night," I whispered, and I turned to leave reluctantly.

Chapter 24

I don't think I touched the ground for the next couple of days. That was one of those once-in-a-lifetime feelings. I was filling my journal and Liz's ear with all my crazy thoughts and feelings. She finally confessed she was falling for my brother. I tried to warn her, but I think it fell on deaf ears. He did seem a little different now, sounds like he really likes her. He was really working hard to walk better when I saw them in the rehab room at the hospital. His nurses said they thought Liz was good for him. He was kind of depressed before he met her. She seemed to help him forget. Lucky for him, she was one of those blessings.

I was busy at work. I had also had Aunt Mags help me fix that Tiramisu that Pops had told me about at graduation, the one with the hooch. That would be our dessert. I was taking on a new role at work, so I had to prepare early this morning, then head to work.

My new role was a big deal. Mrs. Songer was grooming me for manager. She was getting older and wanting to step back from coming into the store every day. I was glad she trusted me and believed I could handle this huge responsibility, for someone who has never done this type of work before. I was so busy I had forgotten it was already Thursday. We had a practice session with the band yesterday, but no sight of Ben. The nurses said he had taken the day off. They said he never takes the day off. *I wonder why he took the day off*, I thought to myself. Closing time and all the girls were getting their things and leaving. I locked the door behind them and noticed Ben drive up as I locked the door. I smiled, held up my finger, and told him to wait just a minute. I went in the back and locked everything up and gathered my things and headed out the door. He was sitting on the bench just outside the store. He walked toward me and gave me a kiss on the cheek.

"How was your day?" he asked.

"It was good. Mrs. Songer, the lady that owns the store, is training me to be the manager. I have no experience except my love of fashion, but she said she sees something in me. So she is giving me a chance. It is scary but fulfilling when someone trusts you with something they have built from the ground up, like their child."

"Yeah, that is how I feel about being a doctor. People trust me, and when I can help them, it is the best, so fulfilling. But it is scary, now that I am a surgeon and actually hold their lives in my hands. I have to care for not only the patient but consider the family that is also putting their trust in me to fix their son, daughter, husband, or wife, lots of pressure. But I would not trade where I am now for the world."

"I really admire you for being willing to do that difficult job. I can't imagine the pressure," I said. We reached the market and grabbed tomatoes, onions, garlic, fresh herbs. We even found some fresh-made noodles. I mentioned a bakery that had the most incredible bread. We stopped and picked up a loaf. Then we headed to Aunt Mags. We arrived and unloaded the car. Miss Millie had left for quilting group.

Aunt Mags was headed to the hospital, and Liz was riding along because she wanted to see Mickie. They would be back in a couple of hours. We had the kitchen all to ourselves. He was the chef, and I was his assistant. He wanted to teach me the family recipe. I told him I was not the most experienced cook. He said he would show me "*bellezza della cucina*," the beauty of cooking. His mother was a very good cook and taught him all she could before she passed. He adored his mother and sounds like she adored him as well.

He was cutting up the vegetables and showing me how to cut them properly too. He had me smell the fresh herbs and garlic. We roasted the tomatoes and garlic, drizzling olive oil over them and some salt and pepper. He said simple seasoning was the best so you could enjoy all the freshness of the ingredients. We would have to wait until the roasting was done to finish the sauce. We put the noo-dles on to boil. He said, "You want the water as salty as the sea."

We sat at the big kitchen table where Aunt Mags had set out her Italian dishes. They were so colorful. She had brought an old bottle of wine up from the cellar that she said was excellent with Italian food, cabernet sauvignon. I was not much on wine. I preferred sweet tea, but I thought I would try. I drank a little. But then I said, "I am going to grab some sweet tea. I am not a big wine drinker."

He said, "Well, to be honest, neither am I." We laughed. I poured us some sweet tea. We toasted to the evening and the show that was happening tomorrow night. We talked, we laughed, we shared some of our past. I told him about Luke. I told him about my family. He told me about his mother and his dad who was a navy veteran. He still lived on Daniel Island in the old house they loved. They had a tense relationship, but he still loved him. We shared years' worth of experiences in those couple of hours, effortless and comfortable. We made the spaghetti, probably the best thing I had ever eaten. The fresh ingredients and the wonderful company I am sure had every-thing to do with it. The fresh bread to soak up the tomatoes and olive oil was just heavenly. While we cleaned up the kitchen, I told him the story about my brother and the cookies he made that almost killed my pops. We laughed so hard. I did not want the evening to end. We decided to go for a walk in the gardens so we could make room for dessert.

Chapter 25

"Anyone seen my coat?" I asked as I peeked my head in the kitchen.

"Hey you, don't leave us hanging?" Aunt Mags said.

"Whatever do you mean?" I said innocently.

"You coat is in the front living room."

"Okay, hold on." I ran to grab my coat. I came back in the kitchen and started telling them about the evening. "It was so perfect. I am totally falling for him."

Aunt Mags said, "Yeah, there is no doubt. It's about time. At least come down long enough to eat something. You have a big evening, and we don't need you swooning on stage in front of all those people." She laughed.

"Okay, give me some toast," I said. I grabbed the toast and the spoon with the homemade orange marmalade and smeared on a big spoonful, then jumped up to head to the garden. "Where are you going?" Aunt Mags said.

"I want to take a few minutes to read Rebecca's letters before I head to work. I almost forgot about them in all the excitement." I sat down in the garden to read one of Rebecca's letters. It was short and sweet. She just wanted to drop me a line. But the second one seemed to have a little more content. Maybe it was about her fella.

Dear Katie,

I hope you are well. It was great to hear about your job and that you have a diner close by so you can get our favorite meal and reflect on old times. That seems like a lifetime ago now. So much has happened. I have been seeing more of our friends come through here at the hospital. Most of them are recovering well. Stanley Ross, Jenny's brother, came through the other day. He was pretty banged up, but they say he will be okay. He lost an arm and will be heading back home once he has his rehab time here. I miss our town and all of its quiet and simple ways. I really miss you too. I have so much to tell you. Remember I told you about the John Doe they had not identified I befriended. They figured out his identity finally. There were a few possible soldiers. It could be, but his dad came and was able to identify him. He still has no memory. It is really a hard situation for everyone involved. We spent a lot of time together and have fallen for each other. That is not the hard part. That is the easy part. That was effortless. The hard part came when we learned his identity. I'm not sure how to say this but to just say it. John Doe is Luke. He was badly burned in the fighting, and with his loss of memory, it was hard to identify him. I wrestled with when and how to tell you. That is why I had not reached out to you before now. He has no idea who I am except the nurse who cared for him, and now he has feelings for, as I do for him. I feel like I betrayed you, but I had no idea it was Luke. I fell in love with who he is now, not who he was then. I honestly don't know what to do. You know me, I am usually so sure and can make decisions on a dime. But I am not sure how to navigate this situation. I wanted to let you know because they are sending him home in the next couple of weeks, and I wanted you to know before you found out some other way. We are moving back home near my parents' old house. The doctors think it might help to be near

his dad where he can heal and maybe get some of
his memory back. I am so sorry this is happening. I hope you can forgive me. Forgive us.

I am numb, not sure what to feel. I dropped my hands and
the letter and stared at the ground. I could not form any thoughts.
Grabbing the letter, I walked back inside, handed Aunt Mags the
letter, and sat down at the table. Aunt Mags said happily, "How is
Rebecca?" All I could do was point at the letter and stare. She looked
at me puzzled. As she started reading and got to the worst part, she
said, "Oh, Katie, This is unbelievable." She put her hand to her head,
like she was trying to sort it out. I don't know what to say. I don't
know whether to be mad or happy for them. He has no memory, so
he does not know it is Rebecca. Even at that, we said we would see
how things worked out after he got back. Guess they worked themselves out, all right. I just...I can't even cry. Aunt Mags came over
and sat next to me on the bench seat. She put her arm around me,
knowing I am in shock. I stood up. "I need to go to work. I have to
get the shop open." I said, still in a daze.
"Do you want me to drive you to town?" she said.
I said, "No, I need to think. I need to process all of this."
The day went by, and I do not remember a thing about it. I was
driving to the Naval Hospital to start getting ready for the show. I
had to change into my dress for my part and fix my hair and freshen
up my makeup. I had to hold it together, just long enough to get
through this. I did not want all of this work to go to waste, and I
did not want to disappoint the guys. Maybe I had moved on, and
that was why I was searching for how I feel. Aunt Mags had picked
up my folks at the bus depot. The hospital staff were bringing all the
patients in the auditorium. They were packing every space available.
Aunt Mags was the master of ceremonies. I watched everyone come
in from the stage wings. I was thinking about Luke, seeing all the
patients coming in, feels like he has been gone so long. So much has
happened to him and to me. Was this the way it was supposed to be?
Just then, Ben came up behind me and tapped me on the shoulder. "I
brought you a little punch to take the edge off. I thought you might

be nervous." I turned around and almost knocked it out of his hand. He said, "Oh, you are worse off than I thought."

"You have no idea," I said as I downed the entire glass.

Chapter 26

Ben was first up. He played "Rhapsody in Blue" with the band. My Aunt welcomed everyone and introduced Ben, and the patients went wild. They were so impressed that Dr. Ben could play. When the music started, you could hear a pin drop. I watched Ben, and I watched the audience. They were mesmerized. He did a wonderful job. I was up next. Ben would accompany me. I sang "Summertime." Then I sang "All for You." My brother made a ruckus after each song of course. Liz was right there with him, smiling and laughing. I am so glad they found each other. I could see Momma and Pops in the audience really enjoying themselves and talking to all the surrounding guys. I then sang "Sentimental Journey" for my final song. I got through them without a tear. Maybe I have moved on already. I finished the song and looked back at Ben. He smiled and said, "Beautiful." I smiled back. The next acts were waiting in the wings, ready to go.

I went and changed back into my day dress and decided to get some punch and take a walk outside for some air. I walked out into the courtyard, and there was Ben sitting on our bench. I walked over and said, "Is this seat taken?"

"No, it is just for you." I sat down and let off a big sigh. "Yeah, I am glad it is over too," he said.

"That is not the half of it," I said.

"Are you okay?" he asked concerned.

"Yeah, I think I am, but there is something I need to do. I need to talk to you about it. I know we just started whatever this is between us. I want to definitely find out what that is and learn more about you. But I received some news today that kind of threw me for a loop. I heard from Rebecca, finally after quite some time."

"Oh, that is good! I know you were getting anxious about why you had not heard from her."

"Yes, but what I heard from her was something I never thought I would hear." I told him the whole story beginning to end, probably more than he wanted to hear. I wanted him to understand. I wanted no secrets. "I have been thinking about this all day. I need to get closure on this chapter of my life that is still open. Part of me needs to know he is okay." I looked over at Ben, and he was looking down at his feet. I grabbed his hand. "I just need to do this. I hope you understand."

"I do understand, but part of me does not want you to go too. That's selfish. I want you for myself side," he said quietly. "You do need to resolve these feelings or whatever it is that is still lingering. I know first loves are hard. They are never really gone. But I need you to be sure of how you feel about us. I want to share my whole heart with you but not unless you are ready to do the same. I made that mistake before and lost myself as a result. I will wait. It will be worth it." I leaned over and rested my head on his shoulder.

"Thank you for understanding, Ben," I said. My mind is so tired from thinking, and my heart is numb.

"It will be okay. Just rest now. I will be right here," he said.

The rest of the evening was spent with my family and friends, wonderful food, and lots of sweet tea. Momma and Pops acted like they were younger than ever. They were really enjoying the retired life, and now that my brother was safe and Momma had seen him, her heart was lighter than it had been in years.

We sang songs and danced. It was a place I wanted to stay. I sat there at the table watching Liz and my brother looking at each other. You could tell they really cared for each other. Aunt Mags was in full performance mode. She was so happy with the show and happy all the men and women and hospital staff enjoyed themselves, even if just for a couple of hours, and she was part of why they were. Nothing brought her more pleasure. The whole world outside was falling apart. The noise was deafening from all the fighting and fear; but in here, for tonight, we were all happy, content, loved, and enjoying each other's company. I sat there quietly observing each one of them and what they all meant to me. My life was wonderful and better because they were in it. Aunt Mags came over and grabbed my hand and said, "Come on now. Get up and dance with me, darling. Tonight forget about your cares." She threw her hands up in the air, and her red hair was messy and free from all the dancing. She was twirling me through the kitchen. "These are the times you will remember the most" I think she had a little more than the sweet tea to drink. Maybe that flask had made an appearance in her apron pocket again. I love my family.

Chapter 27

It had been a couple of days since the show. My parents went back home, my brother back at the hospital, just for a few more weeks. Then they said he could go home. I think Liz was moving back with him. They would stay with Momma and Pops. They had plenty of room in that enormous house. I was busy with work and hadn't seen Ben since the evening of the show. I thought it best to put some space between us so I could clear my head and figure out how to go forward. I decided one evening I should write Rebecca back. I am sure she was wondering about my silence. How do I start this letter? What am I going to say? Well, here we go.

Rebecca,

How do I respond to something so incredible? My first thought was numb. It was such an unbelievable story. After the shock of it all, I had time to think about how I really felt. I would like to see you both when you come back home. On your way back, could you can stop in Charleston, and we can meet at that diner I told you about. I am still not totally sure how I feel, but I know I need to resolve that chapter I never really closed with Luke. I hope he is doing well, and I am glad he has you there even though he does not know who you are from his past. I am not sure what else to say right now. But I hope you will agree to meet me when you get back to town. I think it might help me move on.

Katie

I wrote as much or as little as I could in the letter. I am really still at a loss for words on how to handle all of this. I heard back from her. They would meet me at the diner in two weeks for dinner. She said she told him they were meeting a friend of hers from school before heading home. This may be the hardest thing I ever do. I am not only losing a friend but someone I loved deeply, and yet they are physically still here.

The day finally came. I drove to the diner and parked just across the street. I knew I would not be actually eating dinner. I just wanted to vomit. I grabbed a gardenia from the bush just outside the shop. Hopefully that would trigger something with Luke. I placed it in my hair. It kind of felt like he was already gone, possibly because I moved on some myself. But I still needed to see him and get this closure. I walked in to the diner, sitting at one of the tables toward the back. He was seated with his back to me, and I could see Rebecca when I walked in. She perked up and had a slight smile. I could tell she was glad to see me. It was hard to admit, I had missed her too. We were best friends. That would never change but possibly a different kind of friendship, someday.

I reached the table, sat down, and we exchanged a little small talk, the typical "How are you? How is the family? How is your brother, your mom, and dad?" It was awkward and tense, not knowing what to expect. Luke was badly burned, still partially bandaged and did not say much. He smiled a couple of times, being polite while two friends reconnected.

He does not recognize me at all. I see how he looks and acts with Rebecca. You can tell he cares for her. It is breaking my heart. Rebecca excused herself for a minute. Luke looked at me while we sat at the table in an awkward silence, not sure what to say. After all, I was a stranger to him now. I searched his eyes and his face for any recognition. He noticed the flower in my hair. He says, "Is that a gardenia?"

To kind of break the silence. I said, "Yes, it is," anxiously thinking to myself, *It worked. He is going to remember!*

But he looks over at Rebecca. You could see the anticipation on his face at the sight of her as she walked back to the table. He smiled lovingly at her and said, "I love those flowers. They smell so good, especially in the warm summers." I searched his eyes looking for any recognition, but there was nothing. He was gone. The Luke I lost my heart to was gone. I had been wiped from his memory. While I was fighting back tears, Rebecca sat back down and tried not to look at Luke or me. He reached for her hand as she sat down, trying to hide how she felt from me. But I could feel it, I could see it.

I politely said, "I need to get back to town for rehearsal for the weekend show at the hospital." I felt a little betrayed but trying to understand since Luke had no memory of me at all.

Rebecca said, "I'll be right back. I am going to pay the check. I have a couple of things to grab in the pharmacy." I think she was giving me room to say goodbye.

I gathered my things, then removed the flower from my hair and gave it to Luke. "Wonderful to meet you, Luke. I know you don't remember me, but I'll remember you, always." He looked at me confused. "Rebecca is one in a million. I hope you find happiness and peace."

"Thank you," he said in a puzzled voice. I reached over and gave him a kiss on the cheek. Rebecca came back to the table with a look of pain and longing to ask forgiveness. I was trying to fight tears and understand, but I just had to get out of there. I could not think, it was all so surreal.

I paid the check and ran out the door. I got to my car and let go. All those memories I pushed back for the last year and a half came flooding back like a tidal wave. The tsunami of memories I wished would have hit Luke now consumed my head and heart. Then suddenly, I see a hand appeared in my side window with a single gardenia. I slowly looked up, with tears streaming down my cheeks.

It is Ben. I got out of the car and walked into his arms. He said, "I thought you might need a shoulder."

I said, "I am so glad you are here. I'm not okay, but I will be. Just trying to process all of this, I think I need time to grieve. It feels like someone died. He is gone. He is really gone, replaced by someone I never knew." I reflected in disbelief.

He took my hand. He said, "Let's take a walk." We walked a little ways down the street to one of the city gardens and found a bench to sit on. "I understand how you feel. I can tell you when my mother died, that loss feels so empty. It's like reaching out in the dark for something and never finding it. Eventually you will open your eyes and your heart and stop reaching out for what is not there anymore. You will start looking for the people that are still here. You will heal. You will be happy again. Just give it time. We can honor those we lost by being those things we loved the most about them. They would want us to remember them and be happy."

I just leaned over and cried. He just held me and let me find comfort there in his arms. He whispered, "I will be here waiting."

Chapter 28

I started my journey with questions, in search of answers. You may not get the answers you want. You may not end up where you thought you were going, but you will always wind up where you were meant to be. For me, this was not the end of a chapter but the beginning of a beautiful new one.

Time once again flew by. It had been a few months, now early fall. You could feel the cooler breezes blowing in. The shows we put on went on for a several more weeks. It was such a help to so many staff members and the men and women that came through the hospital during that time. My brother and Liz had been back home for a while and were engaged and planning their wedding. Her parents had finally made it over here from London and decided to stay for a while. They really hit it off with Momma and Pops. I was now managing the shop full-time. This opportunity came around when I needed something to concentrate on, to focus my direction. I moved out of the B&B. Aunt Mags picked up work from the connections she made at the hospital. She became the haven for some, when they had an injured family member in the Naval Hospital. She was able to provide transportation and comfort for them when they were away from the hospital. She truly found her calling. My place was in Charleston. It was a small flat but so close to work and all the activity downtown. Ben purchased a house on Sullivan's Island. It was beautiful. We were planning the trip back home for the wedding.

It was set for the end of September. I had been working with Liz on getting everything together. It was going to be a simple ceremony on the dunes near the beach. We would have a reception at the house. Momma and Aunt Mags was cooking the meal and the cake. I could not wait to help with all the delicious food. I was also looking forward to taking Ben home to see all the places he only heard about from all of my rambling conversations. I was asked to be the maid of honor, and Ben was the best man. I had found a dress, and we located a suit for Ben. It was not a tuxedo affair but a much more casual event. They ordered the wedding dress, and I was bringing it with me to the house, after being altered. It was beautiful and perfect for her tiny frame.

It was the day before the wedding, and we arrived at my parents' house in the late morning. They were putting up a few decorations on the porch and hung the twinkling lights in the big tree out in front. I was standing on the porch, leaning up against the post and watching all the activity, remembering my graduation and the big birthday party for Rebecca. That was the time my whole life was in a whirlwind. I had no idea where I belonged or where I would be going next. I found a peace and contentment where I was now. I knew what I wanted and had an idea about where I was headed, relatively. I did not see any tunnels or forks in the road so far. It appeared to be a straight stretch of road ahead.

I went to my room and pulled out my journal. When I picked it up, a few things fell out, the gardenia that Luke had given me on the truck ride home and a small paper that had been folded and not looked at in quite some time. I opened it up. It was the note that Luke left on my window sill before he left the last time I saw him. It simply said, "I'll Remember You." Maybe, somewhere deep down inside, I am still there as a small memory, and I was okay with that now.

I had picked up the newspaper as I headed down the stairs. I grabbed some sweet tea from the kitchen and went out to the porch where everyone else already gathered, laughing and talking. My Aunt Mags stood at the end of the porch smoking, isolating from everyone in the shadows as she often did, enjoying a quiet moment. I walked over and sat down in the chair near her. She said, "Hey Katie, what are you up to? I see you found the paper."

"Yes, why?" I said.

She said, "Take a look at page four."

"Okay?" I said curiously. There on the page was a pic of Rebecca and Luke. It was their engagement announcement. Rebecca looked beautiful. I cannot say I was surprised. "I am actually happy for them. They both deserved to be," I said.

"Wow, you took that well," she said. "Yeah, I have had time to really think about it, and I think things worked out for the best. I was sad and went through all the emotions, but in the end, I think it all worked out the way it was meant to be." It is like that was another life.

Ben walked up and said, "Are we ready to go?"

I jumped up and said, "I sure am. Let's get you back on a bike." He rolled his eyes. I looked at Aunt Mags and said, "He is not looking forward to this. He has not been on a bike since he was a kid." I smiled at him and gave him a push. "I am taking him on a tour of my old haunts, so he can see where all my stories are coming from."

We headed to the old shed to dig out the bikes. He located my brother's old bike with the flames, and I found my old trusty bike with the basket still attached. We cleaned them up and gave them a little fresh grease on the chains, and off we went. He was very wobbly and slow at first, but then he started to get a little better after a ride around the block. I thought that would be best before we headed into town. I can't be seen with someone who needs training wheels. By the time we were a few blocks away, he found his groove and wanted to race me. It was a perfect day for riding, and I took him by the church and old high school. We stopped to see Mrs. Vance and told her that I was the manager of a shop. I introduced her to Ben. She looked at me with raised eyebrows in approval. "Oh, Katie, I am so proud of you. Remember to share your knowledge. It is so rewarding," she said earnestly.

"I will, I promise to pass on all you shared with me," I assured her. I hugged her, and we were off to the next haunt, the drug/diner. So many memories came to mind. Remembering Rebecca was a little painful as I reflected on our many times here. We walked in, and everything was just the same as walking back in time. I saw all the cooks, and the druggist waved as I walked in from the back of the store. I asked for our old booth, and we sat down. I ordered the large plate of fries and two chocolate malts. Ben said laughing, "We are creating job security for a vascular surgeon, somewhere."

"Yes, but we are biking all over town so that cancels out the bad stuff," I rebutted. He concurred with my reasoning, reluctantly. He agreed it was a great combination and loved ketchup as much as I did. It was a match made in diner heaven.

We finished up and headed back to the house to help with getting the wedding set up. The house was a buzz with activity. I could smell the food cooking outside before we even got in the house. As we put our bikes away and walked around the side of the house to the kitchen door, I heard, "Yoohoo! Katie!" that familiar voice, Mrs. Gottleib. As I turned around, there she was in her signature flowered dress and beehive hair, racing toward me with open arms.

"Hi, Mrs. Gottlieb." She hugged me.

"How are you darlin'? Are you wearing that sunscreen?" She laughed.

"Yes, ma'am, I have Noxzema too just in case."

"Who is this tall glass of sweet tea?" she said enthusiastically.

"This is Ben. We met in Charleston."

"Well, welcome, Ben, hope you are going to stick around."

"Yes, ma'am, I think she is stuck with me." He looked at me and smiled, a little scared he was about to be on the receiving end of a bear hug, and he was right. She jumped right in there. I kind of forgot to warn him about her. We laughed as she went back to her house, and we went in to help with the wedding.

We had a big day, and all convened on the front porch for the evening wind down. Sweet tea was had by all, and I made a lemon Bundt cake for after dinner. The evening air was still warm, with a hint of salty sea and gardenias. I missed that, being a city girl now. I decided to sneak out while everyone enjoyed the evening to head over to the beach for short walk. I took off my shoes as I got close to my favorite path. I crossed the dunes to the sound of those crashing waves and seagulls searching for their evening meal. I looked down the beach both ways and decided to head down to my driftwood log. I got there and sat down. It was so beautiful and calming. I closed my eyes and soaked it all in, digging my feet in the sand. "I read once in a magazine, the sand is good for exfoliating your feet," I heard a voice say from a short distance away. I looked up, and it was Rebecca. "I saw you were immersed at the moment and did not want to startle you."

"Oh, hi." I was unsure what to say.

"I know things are awkward between us, and I can't stand it," Rebecca said. "I miss my best friend."

"I miss you to Becca. I saw your announcement in the paper. You looked beautiful," I said, looking out at the surf.

"Oh, yeah, that was Mother's idea. You know me, I am not about making a big fuss. I am sure the wedding will be a big production too, if I don't pull on the reigns. Do you mind if I sit with you for a minute?"

"Yeah, sure," I said, still not able to look at her. "I just needed some fresh air.

Becca said, "Me too, lots going on at the house right now."

"Oh yeah, your brother is getting married. I met Liz she is really nice." I looked at her a little surprised. "It is a small town… so," Rebecca said. "Katie, I anticipated you would be out here this evening, knowing you were back in town today. My hunch was right. That is because we are best friends. I just wanted to say in person I am truly sorry. I never meant any of this to happen. It is killing me that there is this between us. I want us to be able to get past this."

"I am working through it. I think the farther away we get from it, the easier it will be. Just give me a little more time. You know me, change is not easy. This was a big deal to me," I said sincerely. "It won't be the same between us, you know, not like it used to be. It will be a new friendship to navigate in this new life we both have now. If we are truly friends, we will figure it out."

"Okay, that is a step in the right direction. I will take that," Rebecca said. "I need to get back. It was good to see you and talk to you about this. It feels a little better." She stood up to leave.

"Rebecca, wait." I walked over to her and hugged her. I know she does not like hugs, but she hugged me back just as tight. We both cried. I think this was what we both needed to heal.

Chapter 29

There was a knock on my door. Still fast asleep, I tried to open my eyes and got up to grab my robe. They continued to knock impatiently. "Hold on a minute," I said. I swung open the door, and there she stood, the bride to be, Liz.

"I am getting married today!" she said excitedly.

"Yes, yes you are," I said, struggling to wake up.

She rushed in my room. "I need you to help me with my hair and makeup. I know you have those movie magazines. I was wondering if we could look at those to get some ideas," she said in an anxious tone.

"Sure, sure, give me just a few minutes. Let me wake up and grab some coffee. Here, you start looking at the magazines, and I will be right back," I said. I walked slowly down the stairs and grabbed my favorite cup and got some coffee, straight black. I needed the energy to keep up with Liz. I stood at the kitchen sink, cup in both hands, sipping my coffee, looking out into the backyard. It was going to be a beautiful day.

After I got my morning jolt, I was ready to head up and help her with her hair and makeup. It was going to be family and a couple of friends and some of my brother's buddies from school and their wives. We had been busy the night before and most of the morning preparing all the food and making the cake and decorating it with the flowers she had picked for her bouquet. The house was full of life again and sounds of happiness and laughter. There were times we wondered if that would ever happen again. If these walls could talk, oh, the secrets and stories they held.

The afternoon progressed quickly, and it was time for the ceremony. We were busy upstairs getting ready. Her mom and mine were all helping us with hair and makeup, and we were helping them as well. We were dressed and ready to go over to the beach where everyone was waiting on the bride and company. My brother was still not able to walk on his own, so they found an area that was grassy and flat so he could get there easily in his chair. Everyone in place, Liz's father played the violin. It was worn and battered from the war but still played beautifully. He played the wedding march. It was amazing and very special to see them together. When she got to the front of the aisle as her father played, Ben stepped around and helped my brother stand. He had not stood on his own since he was injured. He had been in rehab and working on it, but Ben had secretly been coaching him too. He wanted to stand with her when she reached him in the ceremony. There was not a dry eye in the place. He looked at her like a kid at Christmas. The love he has for her is genuine. She felt the same for him. Who would have thought, one day she was walking down a dirt road, not knowing where she was going and wound up right where she was supposed to be all along. I am just happy. I was able to be part of it. I looked over at Ben, helping my brother stand, and I had this overwhelming feeling and an urge to tell him I loved him. We had not said anything close to that yet. But I was feeling a release being back home. I think my healing was coming full circle.

Once the vows were done, he got back in his chair, and Liz got in his lap. Everyone was throwing rice and celebrating. We all gathered back at the house. Momma and Aunt Mags set up the cake and the punch there in the dining room. Everyone got their plates and drinks and scattered to all the various places to sit. The sun was going down, but we had lanterns and the lights in the big tree out front. It was a wonderful day. I was wandering through the house, the porch, and the front yard, visiting with everyone. Some people I had not seen in quite some time. Some of them were the same, and some were different now. The war was cruel. I saw some new faces. Some guys found brides along the way. Like Mickie found Liz, they all had a special story about how they found each other. We all started out thinking we know where we are going and who we will wind up with, but life does not work that way.

Everyone started to leave. We were cleaning up each area as it cleared out. I was inside helping Momma in the kitchen. Aunt Mags came in and said, "There is someone outside asking for you."

I looked at her and said, "Who is asking for me this late?" I dried my hands and took off my apron and headed to the door. I walked out on the porch and saw no one, nothing but the dark. I shouted back in the house, "There is no one out here." All of a sudden, the lights came on in the tree; and there stood Ben, my sweet Ben, alone, in his suit from the wedding, smiling and looking right at me. He reached out his hand. I walked down to him and took his hand. He said, "Are you done with reaching into the empty darkness and finding nothing? I am here I want to be your soft place to land. I love you, Katie."

"Yes, I am ready to be okay. I am ready to be happy. I love you too, Ben." Ben smiled and looked at me. I could feel how much he loved me.

"So many times I have wanted to tell you, but I knew it was not the time. I did not fall in love with you. I think we walked into love together, with our eyes wide open." We both had tears in our eyes, saying what we had felt for so long but were not free to express and feel with abandon.

"Are you done with your speech now?" I said.

He laughed. "Yes, I am done."

"Then kiss me, you old fool." He grabbed me and held me tight and kissed me. There was a large collective cheer and applause coming from the house. Everyone was standing on the porch watching the whole thing.

Aunt Mags shouted, "It is about time!" We walked back up to the porch, and everyone finished out the evening with cake and punch and each other's company. We all would be back to our everyday busy lives in just a few hours. I looked around at everyone still there and recalled their part in my journey so far. I have found the love of my life and the possibilities seemed endless. Remember all the pieces will fall into place. But until then keep moving forward and laugh at the chaos, live in the moments, you will want to remember them the rest of your life, and every path will lead you where you were meant to be all along.

About the Author

T.M. Fletcher is a mother of two boys, works from home, and is married to her best friend Dan. She loves cooking and travel and enjoys the sweet and savory moments of life. She is new to writing and enjoys creating these characters, and worlds to wander in, even when she cannot actually travel. She wants to leave something behind, that can be enjoyed long after she is gone.

CPSIA information can be obtained
at www.ICGtesting.com
Printed in the USA
BVHW030809061221
623324BV00009B/38